Patricia R. Liles

Papa's Jade

RoseDog Books
PITTSBURGH, PENNSYLVANIA 15238

The contents of this work including, but not limited to, the accuracy of events, people, and places depicted; opinions expressed; permission to use previously published materials included; and any advice given or actions advocated are solely the responsibility of the author, who assumes all liability for said work and indemnifies the publisher against any claims stemming from publication of the work.

This book is a work of fiction. Names, characters, places and incidents either are the result of the author's imagination or are used fictionally. Any rememblence to persons living or dead, business or establishments, events or locales is totally coincidental.

All Rights Reserved
Copyright © 2019 by Patricia R. Liles

No part of this book may be reproduced or transmitted, downloaded, distributed, reverse engineered, or stored in or introduced into any information storage and retrieval system, in any form or by any means, including photocopying and recording, whether electronic or mechanical, now known or hereinafter invented without permission in writing from the publisher.

RoseDog Books
585 Alpha Drive
Suite 103
Pittsburgh, PA 15238
Visit our website at *www.rosedogbookstore.com*

ISBN: 978-1-6442-6756-1
eISBN: 978-1-6442-6779-0

To my granddaughters,
Regina, Kerrie and Casey
whose papa was their priceless Jade.

Also by Patricia R. Liles

Isobel's Attic
The Song of Sea Gulls
A Bridge Over Satan's Ravine

Chapter One

"Aunt Millie, are you all right? Who was at the door?"

Sondra Powell, an Interior Decorator in demand, called out to her aunt twice from within their retreat which had once been the downstairs bedroom of their two-storey bungalow.

Located on Springerton Avenue, in an unincorporated area of Newark, the small house had been in need of renovation. They had bought it and attacked with fervor, as their finances had permitted over the years. The exterior siding was done in Cedar colored shingles which Millicent had declared orange, but was toned-down by the creamy white trim on windows and millwork—brackets, balusters and arches.

Sondra had not been satisfied until she had directed the painter to add a dark spruce colored line-of-trim in strategic places for emphasis. Surrounded by lawn and shrubs of varying green, and with pots of blooming flowers on the porch, and the front door painted Cedar color around a frosted glass window, it had been declared elegant by their neighbor, Fred Lewis, and his pooch named August who took their walk past the house daily.

Away from the crowds, it was within easy reach of Sondra's clients in New York and Pennsylvania who valued her ideas and her ability to get back and forth without car fare.

"Sondy! Caleb has died!" Millicent wailed. She stood out on the front porch in the glaring sun, among the colorful pots of flowers, distraught by the telegram in her hand. It had just been delivered by a boy in uniform and she had hesitated to open it. She always feared the news which arrived in such an impersonal manner, as if notice of birth and death were mundane events that would require no humane reaction.

"He shouldn't have died, he was only seventy-two," she whispered. She was six years younger than Caleb, her only sibling. A cold chill gripped her despite the warm sunshine.

"Sondra?" she called out again as, groping, stepping indoors and closing the door behind her gently, she was being cautious of the frosted glass window which looked more delicate than it actually was. The window had fascinated her from the first sight of the house, for it was oval shaped, and designed with a perfect rose centered in a wreath of *Passiflora edulis*—Passion Flowers. Involuntarily, her hand went up to caress the image.

From the first glimpse of the window, she had immediately linked the design to the Christ and, although the panel was colorless, she knew the rose was red for the blood Jesus had shed, while the purple ten-petal flowers surrounding it were the Passion Flowers…the color for atonement. The frosted panel beckoned; she had stuck stubbornly to her choice of this mid-century bungalow over any other, because it was away from the life she had lived as *his* wife… Moreover, she seemed oblivious to the deep-rooted sensation that this was a haven provided by God for the two of them. Millicent was not Catholic, she could not have said why she was responding thus to this glass panel.

She walked slowly through the parlor and down the hall, shivering uncontrollably. What would she do? Her brother Caleb had supplemented their inadequate income for more than twenty years, from the time he had given his two-year old daughter into her care, assuring her that he would never marry again. He had been true to his word; he never looked back. Millicent had become dependent on that income as the child grew, and so did her own needs.

Shaken at the enormity of his request, she had nevertheless been proud that he had trusted her with such a precious task. She loved him dearly; Caleb and Sondra were her family.

The humiliating death of her husband some years ago had left her on her own; she had no children, and she had never dared to pledge herself to any man again. Besides, she'd had a wonderful responsibility given to her by Caleb—a tremendous trust that she could not fail to keep.

Preoccupied, Sondra did not fully grasp the distress in Millicent's voice, and offered no comment, as she laid out fabric on a folding table; she draped some pieces on the couch, chairs and even tables, in order to bring together

her latest ideas for redecorating a client's home. There were associated artifacts which she always managed to select with care; now she was bringing it together by rearranging the entire layout again and again. Fully engrossed, she looked up, "I just can't seem to get the look I want, somehow...."

Bracing herself, Millicent repeated her news more calmly this time. "Caleb is dead. I cannot bear it—this telegram—I have never received a telegram containing good news, and I wasn't eager to open this one. In fact, reading it has nearly caused me to have a panic attack." She stood waiting for Sondra's attention.

Sondra looked up, aware of her aunt's distress at last. "What? What did you say?"

"Listen, Sondy! Your father, my brother, is dead!—did you hear me?" Millicent waved the telegram.

"Who? *My* father?—I don't have a father—you mean Caleb Powell?" Sondra went back to her task. "What has that to do with us? He lives in California, doesn't he?"

Twenty some years had passed since the day he had placed the two-year old Sondra in her aunt's keeping, with the admonition to 'take care of my darling, make her the woman she should be for Susan.' Millicent had never questioned his letters or the small income that he generously sent each month. But she did question his failure to appear before Sondra even once.

Suddenly, the only image of Caleb that Millie had of him—his wedding picture—swam before her eyes. At forty he had been handsome and dark-eyed, and always preoccupied with his own interests. But Caleb's marital bliss had lasted such a brief time; his bride of four years had died, and he had requested that his sister raise his child—whether from grief or desperate for someone to relieve him of the task. He had insisted upon sending them away from San Francisco, declaring that it was for the benefit of the child. Thus Millicent went home to New Jersey, taking a toddler who cried for her mother all the way across the continent. A daunting task which she performed to the best of her ability, and which, in time, lessened her own grief.

Nevertheless, Caleb *had* kept in touch with his sister. He wrote often asking for regular reports and pictures, but never came himself, nor did he contact the child, despite Millicent's pleading. She recalled that he was even abrupt with her for suggesting it. He surely must know Sondra needed a father. She was bound to grow up resenting his absence.

Indeed, he made no effort to attend any of the important events in Sondra's life, so it was not surprising that she now rejected him. The one time in her early teens when she had said shockingly, 'Caleb Powell has his *Jade* to keep him warm, doesn't he?' Millie had realized how deeply Sondra was hurt by his attitude; still, she hadn't been able to bring them together, try as she did so many times.

Millicent had chided. "Oh, Sondy, what a thing to say. I doubt she is a disreputable woman. Caleb must have *someone* to care for the child. He was adamant that she was to have knowledge of her two-sided heritage, dear. That's all…." Millicent never approved or understood Caleb's decision, and reluctantly she resigned herself to the care of Sondra—especially after Caleb had informed her that he had permanently employed the Chinese woman, Gem Chang, to care for Su Liu in his home in Sacramento. In the house he bought for Susan. That was the last straw to Millicent.

As the years passed and Caleb remained unmarried, she sometimes wondered about his relationship with Gem, but the woman had returned to her family when Su Liu, who was now Sue Lee Powell, had become a promising young thirty-something barrister in San Francisco and he had no further need of Gem. He had once referred to her as his 'lucky Jade', or so she thought. Millicent would not touch that with a ten-foot pole. Misunderstanding him, she never comprehended that he meant jade literally without reference to Gem. It was the closest he ever came to revealing what the Mandarin had bestowed upon him for agreeing to this compassionate gesture. Caleb modestly let it be understood that he was simply honoring a desperate Mandarin's plea to save the child. In time the jade was forgotten. Or so it would seem.

In the quietness of the room, they each grappled with a way to ease the tension. At last, Sondra pushed aside her fabric samples and curled up on the couch.

"So, what are we expected to do about it?" She asked. "He is nothing to us. Why are you so upset?"

Sondra Powell was much in demand from Cape May to New York City. Her designs were never from a book, but always done with personal care to the client's individuality. So it was that presently, working with a twenty-four inch marble figure of a Roman maid carrying a terracotta jug on her shoulder, Sondra held a swatch of soft green brocade behind it. She nodded and put it aside. Sondra sighed. The figure would rest beside the fireplace on a marble pedestal. Sondra had suggested something a bit larger would be needed, but was told that *this* one had been created in Italy especially for her client whose name was Daphne and whose la-di-da manner insisted *this* was the one to use.

"So much for that." She sighed. "I don't have to live with it. It's nothing to do with me."

"Oh, Sondy, it has everything to do with us."

"I meant the way Daphne's room is turning out."

Waving her aunt to a seat, she coaxed, "Millie, don't take it so hard. I guess I don't understand, never having had a sibling, or a father. It really isn't important, you know. I am fine with my life. I have you, the dearest thing on earth, and we are doing great. Just look around. We have got us a house and it is so cute and cozy. Maybe someday I can have enough saved for us to take on something bigger, but it will never take the place in my heart of this—our home. You have given me such love, Millie."

Millicent took in a quick deep breath and tried to think. She had never shared her heartache with anyone, and was loath to bring it up at this late date. Back then, she'd just been deserted by her alcoholic husband, Wallace Sherman. She'd silently suffered the shame of his having been found dead in a gutter, the victim of his excesses. Soon after, the fact that she was to become the only answer to Caleb's irrational thinking, with regard to Sondra, forced her to focus on her immediate needs, and she no longer thought of him.

Believing that she was not a natural mother, she furthermore had no place to turn for advice and waded in with all the love she had for Sondra. Perhaps she had been too much a disciplinarian—of course she was mistaken. The mothering instinct surfaced once they began life together in her apartment—across the nation—at Caleb's insistence upon distance between them.

Years had gone by before he finally informed her of his reasoning in the choice between his little toddler and the Chinese child. Millicent had never seen fit to tell Sondra about the letters, so brother and sister had communicated with one another as if Sondra did not exist.

"Sondra, hear me out, please. Your father has died. We are the only ones to mourn him."

Mourn him? Sondra interrupted. "I mourn him? I don't think so. If it is respect you are hinting at, I can do that from here. Some individual out West who has nothing to do with me has died, so I respect that. Let that—that favorite person whom he chose to keep with him mourn him."

Sondra sat up, and pointed to another statuette. "So, what do you think of *this* combination? I like this antiqued golden finish on the maid with the basket of grapes on her shoulders. It goes well with the print fabric Stephie Joslin selected for her library slipcovers. Just a touch of it in this vine, see. Most of the decor is Country English."

"Sondy, please, honey. You look so much like your mother—I have much to tell you, to make you understand Caleb. Do bear with me, and listen, please."

Sondra blew a strand of light brown hair out of her eyes. Caleb and Susan had somehow managed to pass on a recessive gene to their baby girl in the form of unique colored eyes of green-flecked hazel, which the fabric in shades and tints of green surrounding her changed them to deep green. Millicent, to whom she focused her attention now, had seen this phenomena a number of times and wondered if it was caused by something she was thinking. Presently, Sondra pushed aside fabric and turned a hazel colored gaze to her aunt. "All right, Millie, this is important to you, isn't it? What have you to tell me?"

Where to start? Millicent thought for a moment and then began, "that foreign child caused Caleb problems. Susan's death left him with no one to take over rearing her—and you, his own child. It was a dilemma he solved in his own way. He hired a Chinese woman who spoke English to bring that one up. He could not do otherwise, he had made a commitment to that Mandarin when he agreed to take the child out of China. Her deceased mother was British, you remember."

"I don't care what she is. I only remember a dark little girl who used to try to pick me up, I think. I didn't want that. I wanted my mother."

"Oh, Sondy, I know darling. I've done the best I could to mother you. I suppose that Caleb never thought of you as a problem. He assumed I was there to care for you, and in typical male fashion he sent me back to what he supposed was a perfect life without asking. He knew that he could not keep his pledge and preserve her heritage unless he found someone capable of giving what he needed, someone bilingual. He definitely did not want *you* learning…try to understand, darling. He and Susan had adopted her in order to save her life. China was in terrible times, government changing, traditions being destroyed, and all of that was done forcefully. All he would ever say was that the Mandarin's plea for them to save her necessitated Caleb's doing exactly what he did—without hesitation. If there was jade involved Caleb did not acknowledge it."

Sondra reached over and selected a piece of date cookie from a plate on the coffee table. She poured tea from the ceramic pot into a delicate cup and took a sip.

"Priceless gift…how do you place stuff from China above your own child? Maybe the Mandarin gave him something rare from a tomb? Or maybe he just had to get her out of his household, and Caleb was vulnerable enough to take the child." She took a bite and chewed thoughtfully. "Millie, I know what a burden I have been to you. You were so—so frightened at first; I felt it for years, but then you relaxed and turned into the best mother ever!"

Millicent interrupted, "No, no," she waved her hand holding the telegram, "it was not as you think…I didn't know you were unaware of the truth…you need to hear the truth."

"And that is? I am old enough now. What was it, if it wasn't the stress of Susan's death and the burden of raising her child?"

"You talk of your parents as thought they were strangers, Sondy," Millicent chided. "You were never a burden to me…you see, I have never told Caleb about *Wallace*, my husband, nor did I complain to him that I was left almost destitute, because your father immediately began sending generous income for us, as I have told you."

Millicent sighed, put down the telegram and gathered a few chocolate covered nuts in her hand, but she didn't indulge, merely held them distractedly as she went on.

"We lived at such a distance, had grown apart, Caleb in his import world on the West Coast, and Wallace and I in the East. I think he knew about my needlework that brought in a bit of income after Wallace died, but he probably never gave thought to *why I did it*, or even that times were difficult for me. He was my older brother, but he was not interested in my life. So, you see, the situation improved when he sent for me to take you, and he provided for us monthly, steadfastly over the years. It was for you."

She looked at the treat in her hand, reached over and poured it back onto the little dish and wiped her hand with a small napkin. She waited, not sure of what it was she expected to hear from this child of her brother's. She could never be mistaken for anyone else's child. She was just as stubborn and independent as he was. Like father, like daughter, she thought.

Sondra, working from home today, was clad in jeans and red polo shirt. Her hair escaped from butterfly clips placed carelessly, which was unlike her sensibly arranged daily look for the shop. She tucked a lock behind her ear and Millicent noticed the square-cut Lapis ring on her right hand. Should she tell Sondy it had been her father's? She decided not to.

Sondra inched forward in her seat, taking it all in, listening intently, again questioning. "But how can you be certain it was for me? Maybe it was just to soothe his conscience. We haven't heard from him. Were there letters to me? Phone calls ever—no. Nor did he ever visit me, us. Why, then, bother to let us know he is dead? Will it be to cut off the income? Whatever can he have expected from us? To go to his funeral? I think not. It would be like going to a complete stranger's funeral. A waste of my time, and yours. We don't owe him anything!"

Sondra gazed at her aunt with affection, unaware that she strongly resembled her aunt, a graceful, slender lady with thick, wavy gray hair pulled loosely back in a bun at the nape of her neck and soft around her face. Millicent was simply clad in a silk blouse and wool skirt. Often she wore a blue angora cardigan that turned her eyes dreamy blue because of some memory of happier times, and always she wore the most comfortable lace-up, low-heel shoes.

Their bone structure was similar, and like Millicent, Sondra had soft, light brown wavy hair which she could never completely tame in either pony tail or short cuts. She had solved the problem with the decorative clips one day and been content with them since then. All in all, though, it was Millicent who knew how much Sondra looked like her mother.

Sondra seemed to Millicent, over the years, to be driven to succeed. She was strong-willed like Caleb, but Millicent was not about to tell her that. She'd fallen in love, during, then after, her school days. In college it was touch-and-go with a young man named Bradley Young who was going into medicine; however, they had parted ways and Sondra had never grown close to any one of the men in her life since then. She dated often, but never encouraged a commitment from any one of them. Subsequently, with Sondra's rise to success they now had a house, each had an economy car, and Sondra dressed less conservatively in today's fashions.

"Don't be so obtuse, Sondra," Millicent said in a husky voice. "This is from Caleb's solicitor—attorney—who wants us to contact *him*. It seems you have inherited your father's business and fortune, and everything of your mother's will also come to you, now." She sighed, "You do look so much like her, so beautiful and slim, but fair where she was dark…I do remember her so vividly, she was only twenty-eight. She was a willowy girl, and I will never forget her in that wedding dress of white voile layered in tiers of ecru cotton lace, her soft Italian leather ankle boots, and her crown of stephanotis vine and black eyed Susan's in that beautiful dark hair. Oh we did love each other as sisters… but enough; we both know she was generous to a fault, and that *you* are not being so, at the moment."

"Oh Well." Sondra scoffed. "He left nothing for the favorite whom he kept by his side in California and educated to become a successful attorney? I get everything? How delightful. Besides, I can't imagine what's left after educating—*her*, and keeping the woman around."

"You are being unfair, Sondy. He did well enough by you, missy!" Millicent snapped, and then she took her time before going on, waiting for it to reach Sondra.

"We need to contact Rafe Barker. He is the Attorney. She looked over at Sondra and taking the upper hand said, "You need to call early tomorrow."

Sondra stood up. "All right. Aunt Millicent. If it pleases you… Yes, we made it work, whatever he sent—he had no other part in my life. Where was his love, his hugs, his advice during those years? There was no time for us. Where were the letters, the birthday calls, or cards? Not a word ever came to me. He left that all up to you. *I* don't know him."

Sondra picked up the statuette, "*you* are all I have, all I really love. An inheritance can change one's life, but I won't let this come between us. I love you, Millicent. You are my mother in every way, I don't remember Susan as a mother, she is a shadow of something that was soft and smelled nice," her gaze turned toward the window, "You are family. He was never that to me."

She looked back at Millicent. "I think he neglected you, too."

Chapter Two

Suddenly appalled at her remark which had caused tears to bubble up in Millicent's eyes, she shook her head; she was being cruel to her dearest person on earth. Because she, Sondra, had no awareness of feeling for Millicent's brother, was no reason to be cruel. But the fact remained that she was only two years old when her mother died, and Caleb Powell gave her away. No loving father would do that…It took six years for her to realize that he had chosen to keep Su Liu, and he had struck the deadening blow by giving her the name of Sondra's mother.

She thought, I was never given a reason, other than, 'It must be this way, child. You must have a good woman to rear you properly'. As if a toddler could understand and be content with his decision. So she had been trundled off with Aunt Millicent to the far eastern shore of the country where, when old enough to have it explained to her, she grew to forever resent him. Until today, she had not thought of him in years.

At that moment, Sondra was startled at the transient thought that filled her mind, *what on earth did that Mandarin give Caleb for taking his kid?* It had to have been of value…

"Listen to me, Sondy. Grief-stricken at the death of Susan from Tuberculosis, which she contacted in China on their honeymoon, Caleb faced the future with two small girls to care for. He obviously gave no thought to anyone else's heartache. He never did. However, he probably felt that caring for the small toddler would be diversion for me, as well as solve his dilemma. He thought of you as Susan's and, experiencing grief and guilt for exposing her to the deadly disease, he was terrified for his child. When in time he was able to come to terms with loss, it was too late. He had given you into my keeping. Caleb was satisfied with what he had done." She sighed. "I doubt he even considered I might someday die before he would."

Susan put out a hand to touch Millicent but withdrew it.

Her aunt settled herself in her chair and went on, "as to Su Liu whom they had adopted under awkward circumstances during that honeymoon, his efforts on her behalf seemed extreme. Caleb had visited San Francisco's Chinatown, and had hired a youthful widow woman, Gem Chang, to keep his house and care for Su Liu. The woman was bi-lingual, Chinese and English, and had been well educated, and even taught school in California before becoming a wealthy widow. She would be an excellent choice for Su Liu."

"You told me this a long time ago...."

"Her first effort was to suggest that Caleb should change the child's name to Sue Lee Powell, since she was the child of an English mother and Chinese Mandarin, but adopted by Caleb and Susan...now, Su in Chinese means *beautiful*—Susan is Lilly—while Liu is *willow*, so to name her Susan would be to call her *Lily*, and that was not wanted. The child was not named for your mother...oh, I always knew how it hurt when you learned they had given the little girl what you thought was your mother's name. You wanted nothing to do with either of them from the moment you learned of his action. I told you one time, then decided not to go over it ever again."

"Oh," said Sondra, "You never explained it to me,"

"Caleb," her aunt added, "forever preoccupied, never realized the significance of the child being named Sue, the situation worked well; he was satisfied to have provided female care for both little girls."

She folded the telegram and placed it on the table and turned back to Sondra. She sat primly as usual, both feet together and her hands in her lap—limp and still.

"Caleb went on with his life, with only memories of your mother that grew dimmer as he threw himself into his amazing interests. His business, Powell Imports, is located in San Francisco not far from the wharf. He inherited the business from our father, Elijah Powell, since there were no other male progeny to take over the estate."

"As a female, his sister, I was awarded a small sum to share with my husband...anyway, it wasn't long after he took over that Caleb married Susan

Whitaker, a beautiful young woman who was talented, a good homemaker, and the only woman he ever loved. Her untimely death made him more indrawn than ever, he carried heavy guilt that he had taken her to China where she came in contact with the disease. Only once did he regret your birth, but it was because he feared that she may have passed it on to you. When you were two and pronounced safe and sound, his only thought was to get *you* safely away from the exposure to the Chinese environment, but that still left him with the dilemma of a child to provide for."

Sondra shook her head. "He must have cared more for her…but what did the Mandarin give them that was so enticing? A lot of money? Caleb wouldn't have been able to smuggle money out, would he? As it was, he had been given *special treatment* by being allowed to visit China. No, with the upheaval going on there—I cannot imagine it would be anything valuable."

She looked down at the bowl of *faux* fruit on the table at her knees. "Millie, I was not yet born…is anything more valuable than the soul of your own child?"

"Darling, he knew you were safe with me. He was older than me, and always rather self-centered; nevertheless, somewhere inside my brother is—was—goodness. He was fair, and shrewd in business, helplessly in love with your mother who was much younger than he, and so something hardened in him when she died; he blamed himself."

They were silent, digesting their thoughts of Caleb's story.

"I want to tell you once more about them, about your mother." Millicent said shortly. "Petite with big brown eyes, and dark hair, Susan of the brown hair was in love, happy and able to accept Caleb's absorbed airs, knowing full well that his decisions were always of the highest quality. Everything he did was done with Christian charity, although his attitude masked it and many people saw him as far too introverted."

"Susan knew better, and loved Caleb unreservedly until her early death. Had she known what he did with her infant, she would have been relieved, for she often told me she loved me as a dear sister during those years after your birth and her illness when I stayed to care for the two of you. What she would have thought of Caleb's provision for the small child from China I could not guess, and he was intractable. But your mother was not overly concerned with what would happen to you. I like to think she would have been content with you being trusted to my care."

"My mother," said Susan, "sounds like someone I would have loved so much. How could she be happy with Caleb? He was older than she; did he satisfy the longings in her for the frivolous things a young woman craves…was she a good cook? Did she take care of me at all…what was her perfume? Did he give her furs and jewels? Oh Aunt Millie, I do long for her sometimes. Oh! Don't get me wrong, I love you dearly, but I just want to know her.…"

Millicent thought hard for a moment. "We'll go to California and you can see the dear house he bought for her in Sacramento. She did not like their San Francisco mansion. It took too many people to keep it up, there were always visitors coming on business and, as she grew sick without knowing the cause, she found it more and more burdensome sorting out the clients and friends for special weekends and dinners in. Her own interests waned, she could no longer walk on the grounds, she could no longer respond to invitations to tea, nor could she take any interest in the radical changes at home and abroad. It was all she could do to spend time with you."

Millicent paused, remembering, "It was a good move—to Sacramento. She rallied there in the sunshine before it was finally discovered what ailed her. I had returned home by then, and only went back in response to Caleb's urgent summons—"

Millicent broke off, swallowed and sat quietly with her hands in her lap, relaxed, spotted with age and slightly misshapen. "I think we need to go to California, Sondy. It has everything to do with us, you see."

Sondra nearly gasped at the sudden insight into her aunt's feelings. Aunt Millicent had loved her brother very much. She had not complained of rearing his child. Now she was grieving for him. Time to go to California to Caleb's world—and meet Su Liu again. My feelings don't matter a bit. Millie must go say goodbye to Caleb. How could I have been so thoughtless?

Sondra affirmed, "All right, Aunt Millicent. Trystan can take charge for me and close the Joslin account. We can leave in two days. Is that in time?—then we'll go to California. You can let that lawyer know we will be there."

They were hasty days of preparation for the trip, what to take and what to leave. Millicent considered her unfinished journal; she had written of those early days, which preserved Susan's letters from before the wedding and continued up to her request for Millie to be present at Sondra's birth. She would take it along and maybe finish the story at last. And if Sondra should want to read it…perhaps she would have an open mind about it.

Millicent went to the bookshelf and took down the journal. There would be plenty of pages for the coming event, the funeral. And the end of Caleb and Susan's story.

"What's that you are reading, Millie?"

"Oh, Sondy, you startled me. I…it's only my journal of those years when your mother—I don't write anymore. I don't know why I did this, but I am glad now. It keeps their love so fresh in my heart. I did love them so much."

"May I read it? I should be able to get it done tonight. It should make going to California more plausible. Thanks, I'll return it as soon as I have read it. It looks so well written, Millie. Maybe you've missed your calling."

It was late before Sondra settled down to read, and once into the journal she could not put it down. She red avidly:

'Before his wedding to Susan Whitaker in Nineteen Fifty Four, my brother Caleb was granted permission to visit China as a tourist; it had always been his father's dream to open trade to China. Well, he immediately convinced his bride-to-be that to honeymoon there would be the talk of the town, and he secretly hoped to make contacts in that country for commercial trade.'

'Coming near the close of an era, China had experienced upheaval that had begun with the Revolution, my brother recognized the benefits of being one of the first to have business contacts in China. He was most eager to take advantage of this new opportunity. Should the United States continue the closed-door trade policy, all chance would be lost.'

'Fearlessly, Caleb considered the events in the nineteen-forties and the change of government in China. In about 1948 China fell to Communism, Caleb explained to me. Trade relations were nonexistent, so my brother believed he must take action. He saw the golden opportunity and took it, using his honeymoon with Susan as a screen to his real purpose—trade with China.'

'Several decades had passed with China under Communist rule undergoing strife and radical change; furthermore, Caleb believed he could go in quietly as a tourist on his honeymoon, and make his contacts. His request to be allowed to visit was granted almost immediately and they sailed on what he later quoted to friends as a slow boat to China, to its very shores.'

'As tourists, Caleb and Susan sailed away, newly wed, happy and a perfect match. She wrote that he was her flawless husband whose advances were welcome, their cabin was a private suite that afforded them the luxury of uninterrupted privacy. Unaware of the changes ahead, their courtship continued on board the liner carrying them to China.'

'Upon arrival they were assigned a military guide and, at Caleb's request, were taken inland up the country on horseback to a small province, Tianjin, which was still under a Mandarin ruler who wisely understood that the government was inching in and his time was limited.'

'Susan explained to me that the new government mandates declared that their centuries-old, silk Chinese style of dress would no longer be permitted. Under the new regime, black or dark blue cotton plainly styled was ordered for all. The population must be controlled, and children were to be educated in government schools, away from tradition. The people must conform to the new policies. No exceptions.'

'Traveling inland by magnificent horses afforded only to visitors, Caleb's and Susan's escort, a young soldier, left them in the care of the Province Mandarin who would soon have no autonomy…he would be stripped of scholarly recognition. He would be designated landlord—puppet landlord—and would soon learn of the destiny of his many wives and children, and future limits on such lifestyle. It was devastating to him to see his future.'

'They were warmly welcomed; however, the Mandarin assigned them to a remote bamboo house, for their privacy they were told. And it proved a haven of rest after their journey.'

'In two days the Mandarin sent for them to attend him in his home, a most unusual circumstance which they would have been unwise to refuse. Behind those doors was the China of old, surreptitiously guarded from the soldiers who seemed to be everywhere.'

'He sent Susan immediately to the women's quarter, Susan explained, much to her dismay at his pride in so many wives of different ages. Nevertheless, she was immediately charmed by the house full of happy children and their mothers, and kept her Christian sensibilities in check. Susan was enchanted by their traditional silk clothing, their shining hair and round, sweet faces, but especially the shy, almond shaped eyes of curiosity in the shy children.'

'There was a misfit among those children, one pale, fragile child being bullied by her siblings. The little girl was seemingly indifferent, Susan noted immediately. However, being cautious, Susan bowed to the women's ministrations, amused by the giggles from the children who watched her transformation into Chinese. At last, when she was dressed like a doll in her silk finery, and her hair fashioned artfully, and transformed by makeup, the children were sent to the nursery while Susan was taught the ways of the tea ceremony.

The newlyweds were seldom aware of the women who provided their needs; nevertheless, they were always aware of the scrutiny of the guard as they walked the gardens. Susan guessed that Caleb's desire was to make contact with exporters, which he somehow managed to do twice, and briefly at that. She understood the necessity of confidentiality and didn't question him about those absences.'

'One balmy evening they were summoned to the house of the Mandarin whom they learned had dared to instruct the entertainers to perform, for the newlyweds, a traditional musical complete with beautiful silk garments, rice powder and fans. The hair dresser who transformed Susan into an Asian beauty sent her to serve tea to Caleb who was instantly horrified, yet he quickly put on a face of pleasure as she played her part to perfection.'

'Later, we had to join our host and his favorite wife in the wearing of cotton quilted clothing. It was necessary if we were to be in the presence of the school children,' Susan told me, after which they assembled on the grounds to engage in lively games and frolic under the care of a wise, elderly teacher, and the eye of a soldier who had to eat his meal of a rice ball, and tea as he sat on his heels.

'Notably, the pale child was missing from the event. She was not tolerated by the wives and children, but was kept separate, we learned.'

'Weeks passed in tender attention to one another, in the paper-thin house. The women came to apply makeup, and place ornaments in Susan's hair so that she might be like them. For Caleb, they bathed and barbered him…It was all as original as they dared make it; however, there was a concern for safety. The Mandarin had set out guards to watch for the government—he was still a man of respect and power, although covertly.'

There was a blank page suddenly; Millicent continued at a later date. So Sondra laid it aside and went up to bed. Early the next morning, she took it up again, eager to finish.

'It was after the stunning performance that Susan and Caleb met the pale child, one of the Mandarin's children who was obviously part English. She was then four years old, small and shunned by most of the children for her fairness, and grey eyes. Susan spent much time with her, with the permission of the Mandarin. The child spoke only two words of English; mama, and baby, and Susan feared for their lives should she attempt to teach her more.'

'Susan and Caleb gave in to the hospitality, took advantage of their privacy and the guard who took them on trips to scenic places. There were wayside shrines of worship, and both of them wondered if this new regime was going to destroy that side of the people, too. They never voiced their concerns, it would jeopardize those around them, they knew. So, they lived the moments with new discoveries about each other. And loved more deeply each hour.'

'All things, they knew, must end. The honeymoon over, the newlyweds began to pack. They were surprised by a visit from the Mandarin late one afternoon. He spoke for some time with Caleb and, when he left, Caleb had little to say.'

'Finally he managed, "He wants us to take Su Liu." That was all he said to Susan.'

"How can he give away a child? What of the mother?" she had cried.

'Caleb merely shook his head and told Susan that they were being paid to take her with them. Her father was acquiring adoption papers, which should enable them to get her out of China.'

'Susan's final word on this was, "Millicent, no money changed hands. It would mean imprisonment if they were caught. We must allow them to arrange it, and get out of China as quickly as we can without arousing suspicion.'

'That was a harrowing time for Caleb and Susan Powell,' Millicent wrote. The Mandarin and an entourage included them in a march to the city where he was to meet with authorities. The government guard was sent on ahead and the Mandarin quietly placed the child in Susan's arms and stoically walked away. A boy handed Caleb a small leather bag similar to their own luggage, and ran away. It contained all of the child's clothing—nothing of value.'

'Unchecked, they boarded the ship for home, spent the night in terror of discovery, but in the end, safe, they sailed the next day. The steamship captain welcomed the little family aboard, giving no indication that he knew the child was not their own.'

America maintained a closed door policy toward trade with China until the nineteen seventies. Caleb never went there again.

Chapter Three

Sondra was captivated by their story, so vividly set down by Millicent. And she read on as Millicent hovered nearby, knitting and sipping her mid-morning tea.

'Caleb was bitter as he told Susan, "The child's mother is dead."'

'So I asked Caleb, if no money changes hands, what did he give you? I know he slipped something to you.'

'Caleb opened his briefcase of considerable size and took out a terrifying figurine It was pure white jade, an ugly mythical creature that neither he nor Susan knew about. They certainly didn't understand the great worth of this artifact from the time of the Ch'ing Dynasty.'

'Susan had told him it was cheap and poorly done and to get rid of it. However, Caleb hurriedly rewrapped it and tucked it in with her petticoats and closed her case. They took it home with them to San Francisco, undetected by customs since they would not disturb a ladies unmentionables.'

'Susan said it was not in her case when they got home. Perhaps Caleb had flung it overboard one night. She never gave it another thought.' The jade had disappeared.

Sondra sighed and closed the journal on its last entry. "So much for that. So Caleb hid the jade, his wife died when their child was a toddler, he blamed himself for exposing her to TB, and then he gave away his child and kept the Chinese kid. And I am supposed to call him daddy?"

"Oh, darling Sondy. Open your mind and heart. Cynicism is not like you. I had no idea you felt this way. Silly of me, but I just took it for granted that you knew him—how could you?"

"He didn't want to have anything to do with me, Millie."

"I failed you, darling girl...."

"Nope," Sondra quipped, and went to get a cup of tea. "The failure is his, Millie."

The remainder of the couple's story was fixed in Millicent's memory. She had not written it, but it was there to be shared.

"Let me tell you the finish to their story." She urged when Sondy was settled again.

"If you will, Millie. This is important to you, I understand, dearest."

"When they had arrived back in San Francisco," Millicent resumed, "Caleb immediately went to Sacramento and purchased a large house in an expensive neighborhood of alpha-lettered streets lined with a variety of Victorian houses. After putting his stamp on the house, they moved in, and the day your mother learned she was pregnant was a delight to them. They almost forgot the trip to China."

"Except that I was on the way," gritted Sondra, "and they were stuck with Su Liu. They would never forget China, like he did me…"

"They were never *stuck* with either of you. They were generous and loving to both of you. Now let me get on with this."

"You were born when Su Liu was eight or so years old. Due in some part to Caleb's U.S. connections, Su Liu was by then legally theirs. The two of you loved one another, Su Liu was gentle with you and helped you learn to walk and play, and she'd even feed you at times. Visiting nurses had no time for it, and Susan did not regain her strength. When it was discovered that she had Tuberculosis, treatment was too late. Susan died in two years."

Sondra sipped her tea and listened, thinking, poor Millicent, you've had so little happiness…maybe our life together has been good for you.

"I loved her so much," Millicent whispered. "However, she was gone forever. Left with the motherless children, Caleb was frantic for a solution. But it came to him shortly, and he turned to me and made his arrangements for me to take you…I am certain he didn't realize that his actions were wrong, that you would be alienated from him in the years to come, even to his own death."

"He made his choices to suit his fancy," insisted Sondy.

"Not at all, Sondy. Only I knew of the great sacrifice made by my brother in relinquishing his only daughter. I knew he loved unreservedly—you were, after all, a bit of his beloved Susan, all that was left of her, and he must protect you no matter the cost to him. He had paid dearly—I regret that I never made that last entry in my journal."

Sondra may have been safe with Millicent over the years; but she never knew about the regular letters between Millicent and Caleb, a promise between brother and sister. Nor did she understand his complete isolation from her. It was his choice, and she had learned to live without a father. She did not need to respond to this summons to go grieve for him and take over his estate.

"This is ridiculous. I'm not calling anyone about him," Sondra repeated the refrain she had sung to Millicent when they received a follow-up letter from the attorney.

"Oh, darling. We do need to respond. If for nothing else, to let him know you are refusing the inheritance. He has a job to do...."

"*I have work to do.* I have to get some items to finish the Warden contract. Sheila Warden wants several items that she has selected from Greenland-Belter Imports, and I have to go see if they are going to fit in with what we're doing to that massive house of hers. In fact, I'll get going now, Aunt Mil. Be home for dinner, so wait and I'll help, okay?" She went to Millicent, gave her a hug and kiss on a soft wrinkled cheek and left, getting into the white Honda on the drive and sailing off down the street of Autumn Village, New Jersey.

Millicent watched until she could no longer see her. She stood weeping, turned and went inside. She searched out a tissue, wiped her eyes and sat in her chair for several moments then seeming to decide something, she went to the telephone and dialed the number listed in the correspondence.

She was connected to the attorney almost immediately and with pen and paper beside the telephone, she documented his frantic comments that Sondra was a wealthy young woman. Caleb had established import offices in Sacramento, as well as San Francisco, and business had thrived. He had an excellent manager in Randall Everts whom his law firm would advise that Sondra retain when she came out to claim her inheritance.

"Surely she will want to attend the memorial service," the Attorney speculated. "We have helped Miss Sue Powell prepare everything, and we have had the house completely cleaned and prepared for Miss Sondra Powell to live in, if she cares to. She needs to let us know when she is arriving so we can have a car there to meet her. The memorial will be held Saturday afternoon, which gives her the week to prepare and fly in. I will personally meet her there if you will send me the arrival and flight time when they are available."

"I'm not sure we will be coming," Millicent said.

"Oh, but you must! That is, Miss Powell needs to be here to sign papers, either accepting—or rejecting the inheritance, in which case the estate will be liquidated and proceeds given to the University. Be sure to explain this to her; if she will *call* me, I'll give her further information."

Why didn't he leave something to Sue Lee?

"Of course," said Millicent. "I will have her get in touch. Thank you. Was my brother ill for a lengthy time? I had weekly contact with him, but he never said he ailed."

"He was ill for nearly four years, went downhill steadily, and often regretted that his daughter wasn't close by. But Miss Sue Powell was there for him when she could be. She is an attorney, lives in Oakland and got over to see him on weekends. Mrs. Chang, the housekeeper, was there every day, and we had a nurse for him. He was well cared for, ma'am, and later passed peacefully in the night, in a hospital on pain medication. I have to tell you that he left a bequest to you. It was his way of expressing gratitude to you for caring for his child. He was aware of your sacrifice, Mrs. Sherman."

"Oh," was all Millicent could manage as the tears began again. "I never expected—we will be there in time for the memorial. I look forward to meeting you. Goodbye, Mr. Barker."

She hung up, sighed and she wiped her tears. "I will make her see that it is the thing to do for Caleb—go to his memorial and claim whatever inheritance there is." It was not right, this denial of Caleb as her father. *She just doesn't understand.*

The flight across the continent was uneventful. Sondra read a good novel and Millicent crocheted booties to send back to the women of Presbyterian Church who were collecting baby shower articles for a single mother's home. Sondra glanced out often, noted the rain and blue haze of the mountains of that name, which were truly deep dark blue. She kept her gaze down on the changing world below as they passed over Oklahoma and the Zion of Southern Utah. From there, drowsy now, she had put her book away and taken a nap before they reached Sacramento.

"You missed Arizona and the Sequoia's," accused Millie. "It was all beautiful!"

Sondra smiled over at her and there was no further time for conversation because they were landing. All too soon they had collected their luggage and were following the queue of their fellow passengers. Sondra led the way to Information to inquire about a rental car.

As she approached the counter a male in an expensive suit and with no visible luggage had finished his business, obviously, but had settled himself there, faced the lobby and braced himself as he flipped through a sheaf of documents; he showed no intention of leaving. He moved slightly without looking up, to let her step up to negotiate her needs. "Excuse me. I need to have my luggage a little closer, please, could you—?"

He straightened quickly, looked at her with an apologetic look and started to move away. However, he turned, looked around and saw only Millicent nearby with her possessions. His gaze traveled back to Sondra, and she felt the shock of his deep black eyes. "Oh. Sorry…are you by any chance Sondra Powell? And her aunt…."

"Who wants to know?" Sondra asked, thinking no man should have a sweet turned up nose and such expressive lips. She met his gaze again.

He raised his eyebrows, "I am her attorney, meeting her plane…."

"Well, we have arrived." She gestured toward Millicent. "My—Caleb Powell's sister, Millicent Sherman—and I am Sondra Powell. We're going to pick up a rental car."

"No need for that. There are vehicles available for you at the house, not here. I've come to collect the two of you. And save you the bother of all that." Returning his papers to a briefcase and snapping it shut, he extended his hand, "Rafe Barker is my name."

He was probably thirty years old, she though. She grasped his warm hand. Sondra pressed her lips together. "Ah yes, Mr. Barker."

She stared at him, distracted by his appearance. He was certainly not what she had envisioned Caleb's legal representative to look like. His black hair curled softly, those eyes were perfect in his lightly suntanned face which was clean shaven. He smiled as if he knew what she was thinking…one tooth was slightly but charmingly out of line. He chuckled.

She blinked and said, "We are staying at a hotel. I have the address…."

"Oh, no. Your home is ready…The house here is in excellent condition—for the early nineteenth century. Caleb lived at the San Francisco place which he titled Powell House…I wasn't certain you would want to stay there, considering your reluctance to come…well we can take you there if you prefer. Sue Lee has kept it up, although she has not stayed more than a day or two on some occasions."

Millicent interrupted, "I know the houses. They were once the popular style of living. It will be nice to visit them again, but I am sure Sondra will prefer her mother's choice, this house."

"Aunt Millicent, it's been twenty years. We need to stay at a hotel."

"I know you will love it, Sondy. Trust me. It was loved by your mother. She never really liked living in San Frisco, you know."

Sondra relented. "Very well. Whatever you say, Millicent."

"All right," Rafe was obviously glad that was settled, "let me get this luggage and we'll be on our way. It's about twenty-five miles into town, and the Powell Mansion is in an older section of the city. It was once a high fashion neighborhood and, as happens in most places, the city grew up around it, yet these old impressive homes held their own. It's a three-storey Victorian." Rafe signaled for a Sky Cap who came with a cart, loaded them up and accepted a gratuity. "My car is out front, young man. Please."

"Then is the place marketable?" Sondra asked, tagging along.

"Oh yes, but not on the same level as before…Back then there were important visitors to tea, and dinner. Callers came to visit Susan Powell when she was finally established here, but then it wasn't long until her pregnancy kept her indisposed and Caleb entertained business associates at Powell House in 'Frisco. She stayed in Sac to the end."

"And now? What do people want with them? Are they slowly demolishing them and—"

"No! Oh no. In fact they are much in demand. Wait until you see the Painted Ladies of 'Frisco…all in a row…Victorian mansions restored and occupied by young couples and families. It may not be Caleb and Susan's generation, but the moderns love them, too."

"My Aunt Millicent has told me their story. I do look forward to seeing the places. I am an Interior Decorator. I can appreciate any period in housing…How often does Sue Lee Powell visit the houses? Will she be living here also—staying for the memorial service which is only a few days away?"

"Sue has her own place in 'Frisco. She will be here with you only as long as you would like her to; she hopes you will want to get acquainted, and that she can be of help to you as you take over the estate, and everything."

"Why," Sondra probed, "didn't her father leave all of this to her? She was here for him, as I understand it. I was not. He never...well—have you read the will yet?"

"No need. We'll observe that formality later. Caleb set it up in trust for you when you were born. You only need to take possession."

"A trust? Everything? For me? I didn't know—"

Millicent was back, approaching from the restroom. "We're ready to go, Millie, we're going to mother's house. I imagine it is horribly out of date, but whatever."

Rafe Barker took Sondra by the arm and began urging her away, "This way...I'd really like you to call me Rafe. Everybody does; friends, that is. Will we be friends, Sondra Powell?"

"That would be nice." Sondra stopped to wait for her aunt to catch up.

Chapter Four

Rafe Barker gallantly opened the doors for Sondra and Millicent. He first put Millie in the back of his new Oldsmobile 98, and then he rushed around the car to settle Sondra in the front. There was a lingering scent of some light cologne, and she wondered if he had a wife who had been dropped off while he continued on to the airport.

"My goodness, this is luxurious," Millie said. "It's new, I think. And large enough for your family, I would imagine."

"Yes, it is new Mrs. Sherman. I bought it a week ago." He eased out into the freeway traffic. "I don't have a family, ma'am. No wife or children."

"You've plenty of time for that. Are you partial to white? And what is that rack on the back for? Is it what they call a spoiler?"

"It's a pull-down trunk lid—and that works as a spoiler in some instances. It has anti-lock brakes, front wheel drive, and comes in 110 at 4800 rpm…I kind of wanted to try a diesel, but they dropped them this year. I sure hope they come back with it. Diesel fuel is much cleaner and cheaper."

Millicent sat forward, "Is that all the stuff I would ask for if I were shopping for even a modestly priced car?"

Sondra listened to them, amused at her aunt. Millicent had no intention of purchasing a car. So why the interest in this man and his car? Sondra looked over at him, then realized he was looking at Millicent in the rearview mirror, as he ran a hand over his hair.

California traffic was heavy but she was used to driving in such conditions…the eight-lane divided highway *was* crowded, there were rice fields that seemed out of place to her, and notably were the tree-lined rivers which converged in Sacramento. None of it was familiar, even though she had been born in this place, it held no memory for her. Suddenly they were exiting the Interstate and cruising into the city. "Trees," she whispered.

Rafe grinned over at her, "sometimes it is called River City. I call it the city of trees. But I like living here. It's alive, and throbbing night and day with activity. We get heat but cool off at night with Delta breezes…a little something for everyone."

"I intend to enjoy the visit," Sondra asserted.

He turned back to his task. "Visit? Only a visit? Aren't you eager to see your sister after all these years? She is a fine person, and is looking forward to your coming."

Before Sondra could reply, Millicent leaned forward, "Will Sue Lee be here? I remember that she was a dainty little child. She looked a great deal like her mother, a British lady, I understood. But she had such a charming tilt to her eyes. Poor little thing tried so hard to please everyone. I often wondered if she overcame her heritage and thrived in Caleb's care—will we meet the Chinese woman, Gem I think it was."

"No, I think not. Mrs. Chang came the last time to prepare the house for your arrival. She has gone on back to Oakland and her relatives where she's caring for an elderly couple these days. She was such a gracious person. Caleb trusted her with everything, and seldom was in town to visit. He spent most of his time in 'Frisco. Sue Lee told me it was too painful here for him. He never quite got over the loss of his wife…that was some dedication, I understand."

"No," agreed Millicent. "He never got over losing her and—he wrote religiously and often called. But he never came in person to visit us. I often wonder at the responsibility he placed upon me…but sadly, he will never know whether I did the job satisfactorily or not."

Rafe turned abruptly into the driveway of a huge imposing Victorian manor with manicured lawns surrounding it. He stopped half way to let them get a first look at the inheritance. "This is the Sacramento Powell Mansion, Sondra. I hope you like it, and will be pleased at what your father has amassed and left to you."

She started to deny Caleb once more; yet she was stunned at the size of it all, and could not comment. Definitely in excellent condition, the house was so somber looking in dark colors of the past—green, grey, and burgundy.

Immediately she felt a challenge. She would have it painted, and probably redecorate the interior. Her mind was filled with colors, fabrics, area rugs and draperies. She would bring it into the century, but keep the ambience. The surround porch deserved a better look than burgundy paint on the delicate, lacy millwork. She would give it dignity....

"Your mind is going elsewhere, Miss Powell."

"What? No. Well, yes I guess so. Is the interior as dark and gloomy as the outside? Are there regulations that prevent redecorating? It would be depressing to live in something so dark and forbidding."

"I think you have to get a permit to make drastic architectural changes in these historical mansions. But that is simple enough. Just apply and wait out the department. They will get you a reply within a few weeks. However, I understand you are on your own for the interior, unless it is on the historical register and open to viewing."

Millicent leaned in to speak over Sondra's shoulder, "It looks the same after all these years. Caleb was so proud of the house when it was new. And Susan was enchanted. She had a great time with Triad Interiors, I recall. They made it elegant for Susan...I suppose it is still the same inside...but I don't remember this driveway, Mr. Barker."

"Please, I'd be happy if you'd call me Rafe—the driveway was added to access the back of the property only after the garage was added. I'll show you...."

He slowly eased the car around the house. Unseen from the street, and across the back, was a dark green and burgundy double garage with automatic doors, and concrete parking.

"Not a carriage house?" Sondra murmured. "He must have added this much later."

"I'll get the doors, Ladies." Rafe offered. "You can go on, I'll take care of your luggage."

Both women took a good look around. For Sondra it was all new, but for Millicent, it was so familiar...after all these years, she thought.

The fenced yard was vast lawn to the surround porch with trees and shrubs providing protection from the elements; it was as carefully landscaped as she knew the inside of the house was decorated. Sondra smiled and walked toward a corner of the yard to the circulating fountain surrounded by concrete benches. Three effigies of nude maidens were posed in reclining, sitting and standing positions; moreover, goldfish swam sedately despite the water pouring from the jug in the arms of the maiden standing in the pool. "Greek Sirens?" She murmured. "No, not Sirens. The gold fish are too sedate."

Beside her Millicent recalled, "Although it has changed a bit, I remember the evenings spent out here with dinner guests being entertained in the waning light—croquet and badminton—and they played until late. I don't think you know what those games are, Sondy."

"Did my mother sit here often, do you know, Aunt Millie? I think she would have enjoyed the sunshine. Did she do needlework, or read a lot. Was I ever here, do you know?"

"During the first months of your life she was too weak to do more than rest in the warm sunshine. A nurse cared for you. But when you were walking and she was chair bound, she loved having time with you out here every afternoon. She would hold you close, then free your wiggling body to go and run with Sue Lee, kicking and chasing a ball…the laughter and squeals were like medicine to her."

Rafe ambled toward them, wiping his brow with his handkerchief. "I worked up a—this is some yard. Big enough for touch ball by the boys if they'd had sons. I didn't know Mr. Powell all that well, he was my dad's contemporary. Ladies, wait until you see inside. Nothing has been disturbed—come along and I will give you a quick tour."

Sondra was not indifferent to the property. From her career viewpoint, she was assessing the era when this house was built. And if nothing was changed, she thought, it was at least early nineteen-hundred. Something stirred in her, a muse who drove her to want to make living quarters contribute beauty and happiness to its owners. The little voice said, 'it's going to cost a bundle to clean this up."

"Is there a budget for redecorating, do you know Mr., uh—Rafe?"

He frowned, "Not for me to handle. Randall Everts can better guide you on the situation with the inheritance and distribution of funds. However, I am certain there's plenty for whatever you want to do. As I said, I will check out the status of the house…you may need a permit to redo anything. What specifically will you want to do?"

"Paint outside. Redecorate inside, perhaps. Have to see if it is as dark and somber as the exterior. Do you know if there are pictures…an album of the seasons of this house? Has it always been this color?"

"I think it has been kept this color throughout Caleb's life. He wouldn't let anyone touch a thing after Susan died and his child was sent to live with his sister…but that's you. Sorry. I can't sort all this out sometimes. New with the history of the Caleb Powell family."

"Then this Mr. Everts will be the one for me to deal with, not you?"

"Well both of us, depending on what you want to know. But you'll get the hang of it soon and can make the decisions. It is yours, all of it."

"Let's go in," Millicent broke in. "You say Caleb stayed in San Francisco? Was it the original Queen Anne Victorian he built before he married? I was there with him for a while, but he sent us here when he had this ready for Susan. Surely over the years he kept both houses up."

"Nothing has been done, Mrs. Powell—"

Millicent interrupted "It is Sherman, Rafe. Mrs. Sherman... please, just make it Millicent. Sondra calls me Millie when she is in good temper, so that might do for you, too."

His smile was not a bit forced, "I like that, Millie. Thank you. So, here we are." He gestured to the open front door; the faint unfamiliar scent drifted out on cool air.

Sondra gasped, "What is that scent? At least it's not decay."

Millicent said "I believe it is incense. It's been a while…."

"What in the world is that, Millie? Some sort or spray or pesticide?"

Millicent laughed at the look on Rafe's face, "No honey, it is a fragrant stick that one buns in a fireproof container. It is spicy, or some other scent used to make your house smell nice. Obviously this was spice. I do detect a hint of cloves."

Rafe grimaced, "I will air the house out. Fresh air—"

"They used to believe the air was bad for furnishings, if you let it in." Millicent murmured. "You know, dust and fumes….they aired everything once a year."

"We are about to change a lot of things," Sondra declared.

The entry ceiling was high, the floor had the dark oak patina of frequent polishing. Shoe-clad feet had not marred this wood and Sondra knew that would be the case throughout. A barely used Oriental area rug set the stage for cherry-wood paneling which, she realized, had been used throughout the house. For convenience, a mahogany side-table held a red crystal floor vase decorated with dragons and flowers, and the creamy jadeite figurine of a Geisha beside it, as well as a guest register, now closed. A Chinese lacquer bowl sat empty near the corner, handy perhaps for keys and gloves in lieu of fruit. Sondra touched the jade figurine and moved on.

A carved, dark walnut umbrella stand hovered near a small bench with a red velvet cushion—for sitting down to remove one's galoshes. Sondy was jolted by the flash of a memory—a woman, presumably her mother lifting her up to the bench, and removing little yellow rain boots…with a tickle and giggles?

They moved on into a large hallway, dark with huge chandeliers from another century. And in that instant, Sondra Powell became the decorator once more. It was a house of paneling, dark and gloomy and filled with treasures, among them several jade carvings. Her senses were reeling as they went room to room, and she made mental changes. The dining room was not paneled, so the dark green paint with cream trim was going to go soft white wall paper with small rosebuds. It would do nicely with the lighter oak floors and the lace panels at the windows. Worn tapestry chair cushions were given a new look in deep rose velvet, which would be at home with the china she saw in the huge China and Hutch. She would keep the paintings and furniture, and decide later which Persian rug to relocate in the center of the light oak floor.

"I can't wait to start…" she murmured.

"You will stay, then?"

"Yes, maybe. I'll stay. If for nothing else than to bring this Powell Mansion into the century. Oh, never fear, I won't destroy the place, just lighten it up with touches from the past."

"Will we live here?" Millicent asked. "Or in San Francisco? You will be head of Powell Imports and have to work out of the offices there, you know."

"That house is where *he* lived; Gem and Sue Lee lived *here*." She said that last as if it were some new and wondrous discovery.

"It's a Victorian, too." blurted Rafe. "Not like this one, though."

"This is too much" Sondra murmured. "Who is running Powell Imports? Ah, Everts, was it? I need to know more about him."

"No problem. He said he'd come up to Sac as soon as you arrive. He's eager to get this all settled and the company settled down …he wants to spare you having to travel so soon again; he'll spend a few days with you."

"With us? Here, in this house?"

"He stays here when he is in Sacramento. It is in the contract. He is CEO, and has access to all properties; it's a convenience."

Sondra frowned, "And everything else, I suppose. Will he resent me? Or will I be no threat to his position?"

"He chairs the board, but he reports to you, Miss Powell. Rand will have to be the one to inform you of the workings of the company, and present you to the Corporation Board as the new owner. It will be up to the two of you to decide if he remains in that position…Caleb put him there four years ago and trusted him to consult on any major decision, but Rand Everts has the responsibility of making it run smoothly."

"Sondy! For heaven's sake. It sounds like you will have a complete change of career. I had no idea," Millie remarked, "that this was so vast an inheritance. Such responsibility. No wonder Caleb never took time to come to us…he was bogged down in this business."

"Not bogged down," Rafe corrected her. "He worked well with Rand Everts. They were quite a team. Both in tune with their objectives and trusting of one another. I am sure you will like Rand. I'll call and set up the appointment for him to come. When will you want to see him?"

"I can't imagine his coming all this way for me. But if that is his preference, then when you call him, please tell him that he will need to choose the day and…he'll be coming to stay in the house with us?" A little note of anxiety had crept into her voice.

"That's always what he does. In fact, I am told he has a suite upstairs…wait until you see the rest of the house."

"But what about housekeeping?" Millie fretted. "Who cooks for him? Surely we are not expected to do that now we have come…"

"Oh, no. There is now a company taking care of cleaning weekly. Gem Chang had a cook and helper who lived in but she let them go after Caleb died and Sue Lee no longer needed to live here. I can give you the name of the woman…she would love the chance to cook for you. Her husband died a couple of years ago leaving her with a meager income. She is a marvelous cook and, if she would get some schooling, she could work in the best restaurants."

"Why hasn't she done that?" Millicent queried distractedly.

"Long story. Bad hip." Rafe said succinctly.

"But then how can she hold any job as a cook? That is a lot of standing in a kitchen, and shopping for provisions would be difficult."

"Her husband was into Alzheimer's and got them in a bad wreck before they realized his illness. Damaged her hip. She had surgery and rehab, but sometimes it gives her pain and she has to take it easy for a few hours. Can't do that in a restaurant. At home she does okay. As to the shopping, she has a daughter who works as a personal shopper…and *voila!* That covers that."

"Is she available to start right away?"

"Yes, ma'am. She went to Oakland for an interview yesterday but the household had too many teens, dogs and toddlers. They needed someone more resilient."

"I suppose we could give her a try. Would you call her and ask her to come tomorrow, if she is available? We need some help, if Mr. Everts is to come stay with us."

Taking a tour of the house next was to Sondra like a trip to a museum. Her training enabled her to fully realize what she had to deal with. That it was a huge mansion could have been overwhelming, but she was more than satisfied that she could make it a more cheerful place without destroying the era.

The upstairs bedrooms were not overly large, but each was composed of bed, bath and sitting room. She turned away from Randall Evert's rooms, the door was locked; however she later got a look, and merely stood in the doorway taking in the heavy dark floral drapery, the canopied bed, beige walls and the use of black, terra cotta and cream to decorate luxuriously. She noted bookshelves, a desk in the sitting room, a black leather couch and chair, and a small round table with several personal objects left there. She pulled the door closed, sorry she intruded at all.

When she returned to Millicent and murmured her distaste at the neglect, she had said, "Oh Sondy, not a thing has changed, honey. Caleb had it decorated once and then maintained it all these years, in memory of Susan I would imagine. He was born in nineteen-fourteen and would have remembered this style of decorating from his childhood."

"He must have had a morbid outlook on life, Aunt Millicent. I can't live in this house without getting depressed. Sorry, but. I will start immediately with a few cosmetic changes… I need to let in the light."

Chapter Five

Rafe Barker had gladly relinquished the keys to Powell Mansion. He had all the signatures he needed, had gotten the documents notarized and his job was done. There remained two telephone calls to make, which he made. First to Rand and the other to inform the women that Rand would arrive tomorrow evening, and Alma Watson would come for her interview at ten a.m.

Suddenly, he bemoaned the idea that he no longer needed to stay. She was lovely. He wanted to know Sondra Powell much better. For the first time in a long time, Rafe Barker felt the need for something more in his life. Or was it someone?

"I'd probably need to get in line," he whispered to himself. "Her wealth will bring them running…not that *she* isn't special." *Why hasn't she married?*

"What was that, Rafe?" His open intercom had picked up some of his whisper. His Paralegal, Nan Wells, was his current interest, after a long period without steady female companionship. He had married at nineteen and divorced at twenty-two, swearing never to commit again. Lately he had found himself resenting Nan's proprietary attitude. *She doesn't own me.*

"Talking to myself, Nan. I need some time away from the office."

"Calm down, Mr. B. We have some serious litigation coming up. Forget a getaway. We can go together, after the court session coming up—oh, Judge Powell called. She and her fiancé will be in Sac next week and would like to have dinner with us—with you. Shall I call her back? Any special time? I could manage to be ready—"

"It will be good to see them…she has a lengthy trial to preside over, so I'll welcome the chance to see them. I'll call her…get her on the line, please."

He sat back to wait, thinking of Sue Lee Powel, and James Kwan; they were a remarkable pair of barristers, and a dynamic couple to know. He looked over at the picture of the three of them taken when they shared a seven day cruise to Mexico last year. He grinned; they would be staying in their apartment near the courthouse. With the Powell's in residence, Sue Lee would not intrude at the mansion that had been her home for many years.

Sue Lee Powell was an extraordinary woman. She was a formidable Court Judge—always fair in her decisions, which may have come from her life in Caleb's care. She was reared by Gem Chang, and embraced two heritages. She melded them ideally as an American, and when Caleb sent her to school for one year in the United Kingdom she was not tempted to remain. But at the same time, she had been reluctant to visit, with Gem, San Francisco's Chinatown on a regular basis. She was content to be one of the myriad of American children and teens who went off to public school every day. Thus, she graduated law school at a surprisingly early age—with honors—and went into the law office of Callow, Penrod and Sykes where she met James Kwan and fell in love. Moreover, at the age of thirty four, she was appointed as Magistrate Judge to the Circuit Court after only four years with the law office.

In looks, she was tall like both her parents, her biological father a Mandarin, and she exuded such energy that she remained very slender. Her fair hair was silken and cut short because of its stubborn resistance to styling. Her slightly almond eyes of grey were her most striking feature, noted always before one became captivated by her unbridled optimism.

Nan interrupted his daydreaming, to let him know Sue Lee was on the line. He picked up and was immediately caught up in her excitement.

"Hi Rafe, is she here? Have you seen her? Is she beautiful? Will I like her…I am so excited. You must tell me, is she happy to be here? I know she didn't want to come. Caleb left her so much to deal with—I just know that he communicated with her almost every day…is she eager to see me, too, do you think? Is she taking his loss pretty hard?"

"I'd say, resigned, Sue. She agreed to come mainly to placate her Aunt Millicent, Caleb's sister. But the mansion caught her eye and she was at once ready to renovate the darned thing. When she gets to 'Frisco, no telling what she'll do. But I would bet she will stay…"

"Ha. There's money enough to do both houses. She will have to deal with Rand about the budget, but if he likes her, she will get all she wants. He's the one who will have to deal with her if she still is not reconciled that it is all hers. As a business woman, she will know a little about heading up a company, but gosh, what a challenge Powell Imports will be for her...oh, Rafe, I am so eager to see her. I did love her when she was so little and precious, when we lost her mother."

She had run down, and was silent for a second. "That was a terrible time in her life. I really hope she will be my sister."

"I'm almost certain the two of you will bond again. But I can't say how it will be between the two of you. I don't think she still realizes that Caleb left her everything. I've learned that she believes he kept you close to him because he loved you more than her."

He heard Sue Lee gasp, "She thinks that? Oh, my goodness. What a terrible thing. She doesn't know his love, after all of his letters and support over the years?"

"Millicent says he never contacted her directly, or indirectly. He sent letters to the aunt, but never talked in person, visited, or attended any of her schooling affairs...all the things a father would do...she actually does not think of him as her father. Was reluctant to come to a stranger's funeral, she said. It's not going to be easy getting her settled as head of Powell Imports. So, anyway, about dinner, you and James set the time and place and let me know."

"I'm coming a day early, Rafe. I will go to the house and meet her. Will that be all right, do you think? I will risk her ire if I have to, in order to see her. But I can't say you haven't warned me that she might be what...hostile, indifferent to me. That will hurt, but what can I do?"

"I didn't see any malice in her, Sue Lee. She is pretty, and dedicated to her career. She loves her aunt; moreover, she appears to welcome friendship... I think it will go well with the two of you, Sue..."

"You like her, Rafe. I hear it in your voice."

"Yes, I do. Now, let me know when we are to meet for dinner. Say hello to James for me. I am looking forward to an evening with the two of you."

"Let's make it Tuesday at our place. Okay? Maybe pizza or something like that?" She laughed. "Seven-thirty. And yes, Nan is included if you wish to bring her. See you then."

Rafe hung up without comment. He was certain that Nan had heard every word. He was determined to go meet his friends without her. Very soon he would have to decide....

Sondra had slept little and was up and in the kitchen searching out coffee and eggs when Millicent joined her. The refrigerator and freezer were well stocked, and they took a moment to agree on a menu, then proceeded to prepare their typical fare, going about it quietly, as usual.

"There's no place to sit and eat in this medieval kitchen..."

It was dark and antiquated; nevertheless it was serviceable—with appliances that would dampen any bright spirit. Sondra had shuddered when she stepped into the room the first time. But it had challenge, was spacious enough to create a breakfast area in a 5-Lite bow window. "I'll get a small round table and chairs for that space." She muttered.

"What?" Asked Millicent, flipping thin pancakes on a cast iron griddle.

"Just planning a breakfast place for us, Aunt Millie. What color would you like the kitchen done in? I am all for a light green with these dark wood cupboards. Beige or bisque for the floor, would really give life to the room. We keep the little lace bits at the window, don't you think?"

"I like the sound of that, honey. Hope the lace is not rotted with age... here take your plate to the dining room. I'll be there in a minute with mine. We need to get done here and finish our tour of the house before the Watson woman gets here. And I need to look at the suite the Everts man will stay in. It may need clean sheets, and towels."

"It's locked, Aunt Millie. Let him change his own linen. We are not here to be housekeepers, you know. We have the memorial on Friday, and then we can go or stay, whatever we decide to do by then."

"Oh, Sondy," Millicent whispered.

Sondra went to the dining room, and judging the brocade drapes over the large window as untouchable, she switched on the overhead chandelier and waited for her aunt; they sat down to breakfast on brocade place-mats at a Mahogany table large enough for more guests than imaginable. How they must have entertained, Sondra mused, my mother must have been a great lady to preside over such a household.

"This was all elegant to the generation who came to Caleb and Susan's table. They had wines, beautiful dinnerware," Millicent waved at the immense china and hutch at the end of the room, "and fresh foodstuff cooked by two professional chefs for the large occasions. They wore only their finest clothing and jewelry...I was here for the last one Susan organized."

She gazed over at Sondra, "They loved her so much. It was not envy or jealousy that brought them, but her own joy at having them here...and do you know, she would bring you from the nursery and in your finest little silk dress, you would curtsey and say, 'good evening'."

Sondra swallowed and sipped her coffee. "Of course, I don't remember these things. So where was Caleb in all of this? And Sue Lee?"

"Sue Lee was not included. She was not able to speak English yet. I don't know that they ever had dinners here after Susan died...at the dinners, Caleb would take you to sit on his knee and feed you little bites of food. He was so in love with you and your mother."

Sondra gulped and dabbed at her mouth, "Why are you telling me this now? I have no memory of affection from Caleb Powel and stories about him will not bring me closer to him."

"Oh, Sondy." Millicent sighed. "I just thought you would want to hear about your family now that we are here to claim what they left to you."

"I'm here for you. Nothing else. When the memorial is over I will have signed everything over to whomever he opted for second choice, and return to my world on the east coast. So, Please, Aunt Millie, no more of this stuff."

They finished in strained silence, and separated after cleaning up their breakfast. Millicent went to tidy her room and do her hair. Sondra took a notebook from the library and made the rounds of the house, with notes filling up the pages. She would oversee the changes, then be done with this house when it sold.

At precisely ten a.m., she left the dreariest upstairs bathroom in time to hear the doorbell, the click of Millie's slippers and voices as she admitted Alma Watson—and another person?

She went downstairs and joined in the interview that was brief and satisfactory. A daughter, Merilee Webb, had accompanied her mother; they were robust women who obviously cooked well and enjoyed their own recipes. They had worked in this Mansion for many years, and were well acquainted with Gem Chang. She'd been an excellent guardian of the little Sue Lee, and hostess when Mr. Powell and Mr. Everts were in residence, there were small dinner parties to cook for, and daily meals for the woman and child.

"We didn't know there was a Powell daughter living on the East Coast," Alma told them.

Merilee ventured, "It was Mr. Everts who told us she had inherited everything and would be taking over pretty soon. We would sure hate to see this place sold and turned into a nursing home or offices, or something."

Millicent redirected them to the interview with Susan, in the library; however, it was she who later assured them of their employment that would continue as Susan assumed her responsibilities in the company headquarters, when she would be held up in San Frisco as well.

The two had left when no longer needed and were living in an apartment nearby. They could begin work immediately, in the face of the unexpected visit from Mr. Everts.

"You are not to worry," assured Millicent, "You will be paid for the full month, regardless of the number of days you actually put in."

Sondra told them. "The menus will be worked out with Millicent, but you will have an account for your food shopping. It will be enough, I think, for cleaning supplies, too. I understand a team comes weekly to do those chores…" She could see their delight at this arrangement.

"They used to deliver our groceries. Just order over the phone and they were here in an hour. World sure is changing, Ms. Powell. We worked for a restaurant for a while and they did deliver wholesale over there…but such a big order was needed."

Alma offered, "Well, we can drive over daily from the apartment. We can be here by six a.m., and leave when the evening is over. There's just the two of us and we will ask for Sunday off to attend church, and Monday to tend to our own household needs."

"You won't find many people wanting to work those long hours," Merilee quipped, "people eat fast food these days. But they don't have a lifestyle anymore for fine dining. And the folks who've got money cater food in…"

"My Aunt and I enjoy preparing our own meals…We are not rich, and do not expect to be. Neither do we care much for fast food. On a daily basis, Aunt Millie keeps us in healthy food. If the hours are too long, we can get you extra help. In fact, if I remain in this house, I may find a housekeeper to take care of all of this."

Merilee flushed, but remained silent.

"Now, we will look for you each morning with appreciation. We've a lot to accomplish before we return to the east. You will be given keys, yes…and do the cleaners have their own? Fine. I look forward to your delicious meals. Of course you will take your meals with us."

"Oh, but—" Alma sputtered. "Surely not with company here. We never sit down with the head of the household. It isn't right."

"I am not buying servitude from you. I am employing two fine people to prepare the meals in this monster of a house. However, if you prefer to eat in the kitchen, I must tell you that I intend to make over that mausoleum and include a breakfast space so the Millie and I can have breakfast there, too. It is a lovely spot, just made for a bow window…I can accept your desire to dine there…but for now we will have to use this table."

"We'll bring a few things, if that's all right with you, Miss Powell. If we are needed late, it will be easier to remain overnight. We used to stay in that little suite off the kitchen…you know, there's two bedrooms and a little TV room and a bath—"

"You are welcome to move in, if that is more convenient. Give it some consideration, will you. We will need you for some time, I am sure. It will take me…well, months to complete my stay here, since I will be redecorating the mansion…we'll talk about that area also."

"Mom—that would be the best." Merilee turned to Sondra, "It would spare us the commute. We can move in this weekend."

Alma hesitated, "Well, with Mr. Everts arriving tonight we ought to start dinner…unless you have something prepared?"

Millicent smiled, "the freezer looks promising. I was going to attempt something. He'd just have to take what we could prepare."

"Let's have a look, shall we," The freezer lid was raised, four faces were reflected in the light and, Sondra thought, it seems it takes four women to bless this thing.

"Well, that takes care of that," announced Sondra in the empty kitchen. Alma and Merilee had departed in joy, and Aunt Millicent had gone to look at further responsibility. She stood and began gathering up the coffee cups and plate with two cookies left on it.

"Mr. Everts, you get gourmet meals beginning tonight. How's that for hiring a cook."

Chapter Six

Randall Everts arrived at four thirty that afternoon. Merilee answered the door, chiding him for not letting himself in. But he assured her that with the new owner in residence he was going to visit as a guest. "Guests don't walk in, little lady," he'd told her.

"You'll be surprised, Mr. Everts. She is a real nice person. Insisted that mom and I eat with the family…we are moving in, too. She, she scares me, kind of. She's a professional decorator and is already making sketches, and ideas for the changes she wants."

He appeared to frown, but it was a natural look under heavy eyebrows, for a man of thirty seven years. He was unpretentious in his expensive black suit with white shirt and grey tie, and had no idea he was handsome. His thick black hair was barbered at his request in an Ivy League style he'd seen on a poster at his barber shop. He wanted no straggling to deal with, he had told the barber. Clean-shaven, his smooth face was the casing for his dark brown eyes which looked at the world with openness, and often understanding. His Welsh heritage was evident, but since genealogy was never a subject in his family, he was not about to concern himself with it at any time.

He was known to vacation at the beach, was into tennis and outdoor sports, so that his tan made him a man to gaze at. He was tall and heavily muscled, never running to obesity even though he enjoyed a varied diet.

Merilee's familiarity amused him. She was so much like his own sister. He would have been shaken to know that Merilee had him pegged as a man of integrity. Her mother, Alma, treated him as she would a son when he invaded her kitchen...

Occasionally he would appear in the news, being interviewed as CEO of Powell Imports with regard to new agreements with foreign countries, and the two women saw him as a person who liked to bring the best of stuff to America, and see that the best of America went out. "It's called fair trade, Mama." Merilee would comment.

Because of Rand Everts, Powel Imports had the reputation of having excellent relations with employees; he would often honor some special person for excellence by making it public.

"It is Miss Powell's house to do with as she pleases." He murmured, after thinking about it. He looked toward the stairs which were visible from the front entry. "Is she at home? I had hoped to get unpacked before we met. I'd like to spend time with Caleb's daughter, undisturbed for a while. But the sister is here, too, isn't she? Millicent, I think. Not sure of her last name."

"Yes, sir. They are both here. Mrs. Sherman keeps trying to tell her stories about her childhood and she gets mad about it. I think maybe she didn't want to come. It's like Miss Powell doesn't like Caleb—and he was her daddy. But, who knows what happens in families...come in, bring your cases and I'll see you to your rooms. We weren't able to clean, so if you will allow it, I'll change your sheets and freshen your linens now."

"That would be fine, Merilee. I brought one suitcase for the five days... that should see me adequately covered. The suit bag has three in it and they are just out of the cleaners so they need to be out of that plastic."

"I can do that for you, Sir. Dinner," she said as she led the way inside and up the stairs, "will not be served until seven this evening, so if you need a sandwich, I can fix you something to tide you over."

"Thank you, Merilee. I could get around one of those roast beef sandwiches that Alma makes. Is that a possibility? Good. And the Mango shake? Fine. Let's get this taken care of."

Unpacked and his feast consumed, Rand Everts went down to the kitchen to greet Alma, thank her for the kind snack and chat for a moment. He was always aware that these two women were more than servants in this household. Caleb had depended upon them to take care of Gem Chang and Sue Lee.

Caleb had stayed his distance from the four females, amusing Rand, because Caleb was almost afraid of them, and Caleb did not fear anything that

Rand knew of. Yet Rand would quickly remind himself that Caleb had two special women on the east coast about whom he grieved. The pictures on his desk at the company headquarters had revealed a handsome sister named Millicent; her photo had not changed much over the years; however the girl had gone from sweet innocence to a beauty as evidenced by the new photograph just last year, when she had been awarded some sort of recognition as businesswoman of the year. Caleb had kept an album in his office and placed all photos of her there, except this latest one on his desk. The old man had been proud that she was so accomplished a businesswoman that he had shared the book with Rand, and repeatedly expressed his faith that she could take over Powell Imports easily.

At that moment Rand was startled at his ill-timed thought—Lana Jo's accusation that he was no longer in love with her. She had insisted that he was cheating on her, but he was appalled at that paranoia. He had long ago persuaded himself that intimacy was nothing to write home about. He went through the motions with his wife, but he often wondered if it was like that with everyone. He endured the years of her suffering, giving all he had to her care, encouraging her, and accepting their life dominated by her pain. It took a bit to let her go, when she gave in to her family and went back to live with them. She'd asked for a divorce and he had made a small effort to change her mind…so small that guilt at his failure hit at the worst times.

They had divorced with bitterness, which left him invulnerable to women since then. It was only when she died of the Multiple Sclerosis that he told himself she had not been rational because of that devil of a disease. However, there were times when he was startled to realize that lately he had been distracted by thoughts of Caleb Powell's daughter…No, no, he denied. It could not be…

"Where will I find Miss Powell, Alma? Is she available to meet me? I am anxious to meet Caleb's daughter, although from the pictures in his office, I feel like I have known her for years."

Alma punched down the dough and began forming little rolls on a baking sheet, "Last time I saw her she was in the library. I think she was making sketches of something she wants done right away to the house. I heard her making calls to a paint company, and then she left a message for somebody wanting to know if the house is on the registry. She's not losing much time… says she wants to get back to her business as soon as possible."

Rand felt a punch of shock, "She's not staying? I don't understand."

"It's not my place—well, I can tell *you*—she says she doesn't have a father named Caleb. Only went to her mother's room and stayed for a while. She was going through Susan's things and I left her alone when I realized she was weeping. She has had a big heartache. But she loves her auntie, and they have taken care to keep the mother's memory fresh for her."

Rand frowned, "She denies Caleb? After all his support, his grieving? Surely the two of them are aware of what he sacrificed in sending the child to her aunt. He had no one. He provided well for Sue Lee, but he never considered her his daughter. He was kind, but Gem was *her* only parent...he once confided that he would have preferred having them with him, but his sister was established in New Jersey and he could not bring himself to disrupt her life..." He reached over and pinched off a small bit of dough and tried rolling it into a ball. It stuck to his finger, so he put it in his mouth. "Um, that's good like it is."

"For heaven sakes!" Alma laughed. "You stay out of my dough, Rand Everts. Better get yourself out of here and go find Sondra."

"You say she'll be in the library? Thanks." He wiped his hand and headed for the one room in this house with which he was richly familiar. He had used the desk, and the walls of books were comforting, and the room proved interesting when he was weary and wanted to transport himself to another time and another world for a few hours. *Alone.*

The collection of books had belonged to Susan Powell; she had inherited most of it from her intellectual parents. In addition, Rand had heard about Caleb's ardent attention during her days of illness, eagerly adding valuable volumes which he sometimes read to her while they awaited the baby. After the birth Susan had all she could do to get through each day; however, with the help of her sister-in-law, Millicent, for a year or so, she filled Caleb's life with love. As if scheduled, she had been confined to her room—before she had died in a local hospital within hours of her arrival there...Rand sighed. This was a somber house. It needed something again—love, happiness. Did they truly exist? "I am not an authority on that," he murmured.

He stopped before the door, ran his hands through his hair and stepped in. The real woman was more than he had expected. He was aware that she was younger than Lana Jo. He thought he knew her from the pictures in Caleb's office, but this was a poised, beautiful woman who looked up from her sketching and stood up. She was slender, but feminine in a blue jumpsuit, yet it was her amazing thick, wavy hair that caught his eye. It was the color of honey, and cut short in what Lana Jo had called a bob...but the unruly locks gave it a life of its own.

She laid aside her sketch pad and stepped toward him. Her questioning gaze turned to one of shock, intensifying those hazel eyes which mirrored the blue of her garment. She carefully backed up to the chair she had left, and he fleetingly wondered if he had been the cause. But, he had his answer as, holding their gaze, she used her feet to grope for her sandals and slip them on. In seconds she was coming forward again, maintaining the look, challenging him to remark.

Rand felt his mouth twitch, as he controlled a belly-laugh.

"You must be Mr. Everts. Forgive me. I knew you would be here today, but not exactly when. Have you just arrived? Then you've had time to settle in...I understand dinner is at seven this evening, so if you would like something to tide you over—"

"Thanks, Miss Powell." Rand interrupted, "I was given a snack—by Alma's calculation enough for two persons—and I've unpacked. The suite is kept ready for me so I can usually get right to work...that's not why I'm here today though. I do want to welcome you. I am pleased to meet you. I've come to familiarize you with the extent of your assets and responsibilities...I don't know how much you know about Powell Imports, but we can go into that while I am here. Then when you get down to the San Francisco office, it might ease the way for you."

"That's kind of you. But I won't be staying. I have business interests on the East Coast that need my attention. I'm here to do what is necessary to free myself from this obligation."

Rand was stunned. "But you came...this is yours; it's an astonishing inheritance. Many people depend on their livelihood with this company. There are other holdings that need overlooking by you—only you, as you succeed Caleb."

She interrupted, "I understand you are the Chief Executive Officer. Is that right? Are you not interested in continuing to oversee everything? You and the board—I had thought you could continue without me. You have not needed me before."

"Now that you have arrived, and Caleb is gone, your presence will be needed for many decisions that I can't make. Caleb gave me autonomy, but there are constraints on how much I can do without the board's approval and the owner's sanctions...."

She did not even flinch, there were no tears.

"I am sorry. I haven't said how concerned I am that we have lost him. He was a fine man, Caleb Powell. When was the last time you heard from him? We were all aware of his letters to you, it was the first thing he did at the office, almost daily...wait until you see the pictures he has in the office. He was so proud of you—"

"I've no idea what you are talking about Mr. Everts. I have had no contact with Caleb Powel in twenty years. You must have misunderstood the object of his 'letters'. He gave me away, and was content to live without me. He provided for Sue Lee Powell and was evidently satisfied to have her company. Why would I want anything from him?"

Rand frowned. "I can't believe you didn't get the letters. He wrote them himself, religiously and had his secretary post them immediately. I recall seeing one addressed to Millicent Sherman. He said that was where you were. He was so proud that his sister was taking care of you. He just knew she would keep you safe until you were grown and came home to him. I just don't understand this...that man worshiped you."

Sondra had not moved, but now she took a step forward, anger in her eyes. "If he was so affectionate, why no phone calls, or trips to special events, to see me graduate, to attend the awarding of—" She broke off, drew in a deep breath and leaned against the desk. Her hand went to the sketch pad. "Mr. Everts, he made his choice. I came only as a courtesy to all of the employees to see that the company continues as it is. I want no part of any of it."

Rand moved closer, "You can't mean this. I don't know what has happened, but we will get to the bottom of this quickly. If you refuse your inheritance, everything will be liquidated and the company will close. Caleb was inflexible about having you carry on. He said so often that you were a Powell, and he knew you would come and take over."

"I have never given him a second thought, Mr. Everts."

"My name is Rand, if you please. You are Sondra Gaye Powell, aren't you? Not some imposter breaking in here? Miss Powell, he would have brought you home in a heartbeat, but he was fearful of taking his Millie away from her friends and family. He believed you two were among loved ones, thriving, and that you *would* come to him."

"He what?" Sondra straightened up and backed into her chair. "He should have taken the time to visit Millie. She does have a few friends, but her husband had died long ago, and it was just the two of us, struggling to make our way. We did it too. We managed to get me through college. I got a loan and began my small business almost immediately. We had enough to buy a little house…if it had not been for the church people who love her, we would have been entirely alone. She worked as a receptionist in a small office while I schooled. I went to work waiting tables to get through college…oh some of what he sent was helpful there. I knew he was contributing to our income, it was sometimes all we had for months on end…neither of us dared get sick…so don't tell me how much he loved us…anyway, I never thought of him as my father—I did not expect him to support us. I did not expect anything from him. I did not *think* of him."

"Oh, Miss Powell—"

"I am used to being called Sondra. My Aunt calls me Sondy. Please, we have suddenly gotten into some awesome revelations here—" She broke off as he moved slightly and his scent teased the air. "Names," she murmured, but recovered quickly, "First names are needed, I suppose. Familiarity won't breed contempt in this situation. It's already present."

Rand looked around for a chair and headed for one that was facing the desk. He was feeling shaky. What, he wondered, had gone wrong? How could this have happened? Was the company going to fold into oblivion, throwing thousands out of employment?

"There is the final option then. One that will end the corporation as it is, and leave thousands without means of support. You simply leave, immediately after filing a disclaimer. Since there is no secondary inheritor, it will be up to the courts to appoint—"

She interrupted, "What do you mean, no secondary? Wasn't Sue Lee in the will? Surely your name was on the list? Are you serious that it was only I who would inherit? I know enough about business to understand what happens here. I simply do not care, do you understand?"

"He made no other provision, Sondra. He was seventy-two years old and as bright and agile as anyone I have ever known. He never once thought of marrying again, although many women tried to interest him. His focus was on the business, saving a successful inheritance for you."

"I'm not interested in him. He's not my father. I don't want his import company, or anything else."

Rand sat down like a tired old man, then stood up again when he realized she was standing with clenched fists. "I have to think this over…Sondra. What ramifications—please, won't you give this some more time? You will need to visit the offices, meet everyone, attend a special board meeting, and meet with the attorneys. You will have to see everything, you can't just sign everything away without knowing what you are considering."

"She isn't going to do that Mr. Everts…sign it away." Millicent stood in the doorway. "Sondra Powell is a fine business woman. Her resentment of her father's seeming neglect is my doing. Now she will have to hear it from me." She stood, stately, eyeing them both.

She walked into the room, found a chair facing them and sat down. She waved them back into their seats. When they were seated, she smoothed her linen skirt. "When Caleb asked me to take Sondy he also informed me of his plans for Sue Lee. I misunderstood his intentions regarding a Chinese woman living in his house and raising the child. I thought she was going to be his mistress."

Her hand went up, "wait…I was angry and told him I would return to my life away from that situation, to friends and family on the east coast. I knew in my heart I did not want Sondy exposed to such ugliness. I refused to stay any longer and he sent her with me, rather than have me make another trip. I never told him about my husband, his drinking, his death in a gutter, the embarrassment. If it hadn't been for the church friends…but that is what got us through emotionally. Somehow, years after Wallace died, Caleb may have suspected I did not have much to live on… he began sending a few hundred dollars every month. That got us to where we are now. We both worked hard, too hard I know now—now that I know the truth."

"Aunt Millicent…."

"No. Hear me out. In just a few hours I have learned what I have done. The woman and child lived here…with servants. Caleb lived in San Francisco, with a valet and housekeeper and a cleaning service all these years. He visited when he came for the day, but never stayed."

"He was fond of the girl. He said that she was grateful for his gift to her. But she has her own life. She has always understood the circumstances of her rescue from China. She never asked for him to parent her. He never allowed her to call him Papa. All this I have learned in a few hours; I am devastated. What can I do to make up for twenty plus years of wrong-thinking?"

Rand looked at Sondra. She was stunned, but realization hit and she hurried over to Millicent and took her hand, "Oh, darling. What a burden you have carried. People didn't talk to each other about those things then, did they? No wonder you were so shocked when I referred to Mrs. Chang as Papa's Jade. Remember how nasty I was? It must have hurt you so...."

Millicent placed her hand on Sondra's hair and patted, "You shocked me, my love. To think you knew such things...how could I have done this to you? I had no idea how Caleb felt, he was so uncommunicative with everyone but Susan."

Rand stood up and hesitated. Both women looked over at him, surprised that he was there, he assumed. "I hope you will talk this over, and change your plans, Miss Powel...Sondra. I'll go...leave you two alone—I'll be back in time for dinner."

"Yes, thank you," Sondy affirmed. She turned back to her weeping aunt.

Chapter Seven

In the dismal dining room that evening, the affection between the two women was paramount. To Rand they were typical of everything he had heard about Hilda Powell whose progeny they were. Caleb had endless tales to tell about his beloved mother—over and over.

Sondra was notably subdued. Certainly, Millicent was not shy about asking Rand personal questions like 'who were your parents; what was the extent of your schooling, growing up on a Montana ranch? Was your wife ill for a long time?' Sondra did look up from time to time, with such a blank look he wondered if she had heard a word.

He turned his attention to Alma's chicken dinner, wondering if the two women could cook…the meal was typically Alma. She knew how to put food together. He always ate in moderation and, grateful for the menu, tonight was no exception. He had no intention of stressing his digestive system to the limit as he tried to persuade Sondra Powell to stay with the company.

Women. Lana Jo's parents had demanded that she be brought to them, in her wheelchair with all of her belongings. They insisted that nurses be hired to care for her, using the leverage that as her husband he must pay the bills. Without protest from his wife, they took her away from him. "I'll never forgive that," he thought.

Since her death, each visit he made had grown more awkward. Today he'd phoned ahead, and they were open to his visit all right, for about an hour, just as they had limited him the last time he was in town, cutting short his time with the children he had come to love. He suspected that ties with Lana Jo's family were about to be broken.

He had long ago come to terms with feelings for her. Without pity, but with admiration, after college he had married the girl who sometimes needed a wheel chair, and never looked back. They had bought a modest home, and furnished it before she was unable to walk at all, making certain it would accommodate that chair. They had been the best of friends. Marital bliss was unknown to them, if it even existed; indeed, they did share common interests like Community Theater and ballet for which he'd proudly bought beautiful clothes for her. He'd taken her driving in the warm sun to many scenic places. Then, with the end looming, everything had to be cast aside for shapeless garments that were required for easy on and off...she could no longer do simple tasks.

Enough of the past. Pushing up out of these dark thoughts, Rand declared it a memorable meal. He put down his napkin and stood up. He excused himself, explaining, "Lana Jo's family are expecting me. I will probably be late, so I'll say good night now."

"Then we will see you tomorrow. Have a pleasant evening, Rand." Millicent finished her tea, and placed the delicate cup on the saucer.

He turned to leave. Sondra was not so indifferent, "Who, may I ask, is Lana Jo?"

He stopped and stared at her. "She is, was that is, my wife. I'm sorry, I assumed you heard...Rafe didn't tell you much about me, did he?" He shook his head. "She'd had Multiple Sclerosis since she was nineteen. She died at her parents' home about two years ago."

"Sondy...oh, my goodness. I am so sorry, Rand." Millicent gasped.

Somehow, as Rand held Sondra's gaze he knew she wanted to ask why his wife had not been with him...but she merely pressed her lips together. "How awful for you," she murmured.

He searched out his keys and with a nod, left them to their thoughts.

Rand made a quick trip to the Stamer's ranch style house in Elkhorn. It was the third visit; the first had been to the memorial, over eighteen months ago. The visits were never easy, they left him drained, and seeking something that he had yet to find. As soon as he knew what that was, he was sure the emptiness would go away.

Jahn Stamer suffered Parkinson's disease, and Lana Jo's mother, Dora, had become feeble with the loss of her eldest daughter. Lana Jo's sister, Eveline and her husband LaVar Rood and two little children, had long since moved in with the parents, and made no secret of the fact they blamed him for their circumstances.

Eveline answered the door, "I've had to bed down Mama and Dad. They are not getting over Lana Jo, and it makes a lot of work. LaVar and I still have a lot to do before we can get some rest. I had to get the kids settled down, so you won't see them tonight."

"I am sorry to hear that. I always looked forward to a visit with our family,"

"We aren't really your family. Not anymore, Rand. But I am civil, I have some cake and coffee to give you for your trouble in coming."

"That's very kind—."

LaVar interrupted with his entrance carrying a cup of coffee and a plate and fork with a slice of cake, using his backside to push open the swinging door to the kitchen. "Gotcha some cake, Rand. This here chocolate-cocoanut was Lana Jo's favorite, remember? We was trying to be strong and get on with things...."

Rand took the offering and wondered what to do with it. "Aren't you joining me?" he asked.

"We had our meal hours ago." Eveline grunted.

"I wouldn't want to inconvenience you." He handed back the desert to LaVar and glanced at his watch. "I'll not stay any longer. This is my last call to this house. I will be busy in San Francisco for some time. We have a new owner and much will be required of me getting her in place. Thanks, and good night, actually, goodbye. Give my regards to your parents."

"Well, I never. Of all the ungrateful—"

Rand heard no more. He hurried out, down the walk to his car and with the greatest feeling of relief, he drove out of the drive and just cruised for a few minutes. It was over, he had done it. He would never return to this family again. Lana Jo was gone forever.

Not wanting to return to the Powell's too soon, he drove to the Three Palms Lounge, gave his car to a valet and went in to soft music and restful décor. He was seated in a booth where he ordered a mild drink and relaxed to the musical combo playing the songs he liked best—he looked up to see LaVar standing before him, waiting for the waitress to serve his order. *He followed me!*

"They won't say anything, but I will." He sat down opposite Rand. "We need money, a lot of it, to get over this loss. Them women want to take a trip somewhere to help them forget how bad you did her. I know you got access to plenty. Lana Jo told us about some jade or other. That stuff is valuable, could bring a lot on the market. We could share—"

"It's going to end right here, LaVar. I don't have a lot of money. I don't have access to money or jade, and if I did, there is no way in hell I would just give it to the likes of you all. Is that clear? Now get out of here and do not approach me again. I will have you arrested for stalking."

"We'll get a lawyer—"

"Yes, do that. Have him get in touch with mine. Rafe Barker…I'm certain you know who he is by now. Don't let me see your face again. Understand?"

For a moment Rand thought he would not leave, but he muttered something about "I told them…" and was gone as quickly as he had showed up.

The place was not crowded; he didn't welcome the deep ache triggered by seeing a couple holding hands, obvious of their surroundings. He finished his drink and left. He needed to go shower away the dirty feeling left by LaVar Rood. He was going back to Sondra….

In the car, he again had a strange feeling of fear that Sondra Powell would leave—he swerved to avoid a collision and, on a charge of adrenalin, focused on the driving.

It was well past ten o'clock when he let himself in. Surely both women were asleep. But he found Sondra alone in the library, seated, chewing on her pen and her notebook filled with lines of writing, which she put down immediately; she edged forward on the chair. "I am so sorry we drove you away, Rand. You don't deserve to be subjected to our imperfections, mine and Millie's. Forgive us. I really hope you were not horribly inconvenienced by having to leave."

"Not at all. I took the opportunity to visit my former in-laws." He settled in a favorite chair and relaxed. "It seems they no longer need me to visit them."

"I am sorry. Perhaps I could get you a drink of your choice?"

"Thank you no. I stopped…I had a cocktail on the way home, uh, back here. I hope I have not interrupted your letter-writing or journaling."

She gazed down at the notebook, "Oh, goodness no. This is just a planner for the changes I want to make in this house. I should share them with you, because I am told you must approve the budget for them—"

"I must approve? You can't be serious. This is yours." He waved a wide sweep with his arm. "I can only advise you of the amount you should budget, and perhaps analyze what it is you will change…but no, Sondy, er sorry, Sondra, I work for you."

"It's not mine. I haven't accepted this inheritance."

"But, Rafe surely made it clear that you are the sole heir."

She brushed at a lock of hair that slipped onto her cheek. "He tried. I told him the same thing I told you. I don't want it. You will be in charge forever. If I set it up in trust, right?"

His heart skipped a beat. "You really wouldn't do that. You are Caleb Powell's daughter. And Susan would turn over in her grave…."

"What do you know about my mother?"

"Everything that Caleb Powel shared with me. He loved her with a love I have rarely seen. He lived with the two of you, and Millicent every moment of his life. You were so real…he often talked of her, and his love for the two of you. Of his good fortune to have a wonderful sister to help you become like his Susan. Oh, I knew her. And I thought I knew you. Apparently not." He stood up. "I believe I will have a bit of sherry before I go up. Will you?"

She nodded and looked down at her booklet. "I'm sorry, truly sorry." She whispered. She heard his step and looked up.

He stood before her, "I think you have the Powell ability to protect Powell Imports, and keep it alive. But that is up to you. I expect to show you the entire estate before you make a final, businesslike decision."

He strode over to a huge credenza, opened a lower door and got out two sherry glasses, and the half full decanter, and poured a small amount in each glass. He replaced the stopper, set the glasses on a small tray, and closed the door. He carried the offering to her and handed her a glass.

Sondra held it, waiting. He gazed at her. Understanding, he lifted his glass and she touched hers to it and they each sipped a taste. "It's delicious. I have never had sherry before."

"I imagine you have not had many fine things, Sondra. It appears that you have had plenty of love though. A father who worshiped you—from afar—and an aunt who mothered you. And perhaps there is a fine young man back there…someone for whom you are wanting to give up this inheritance?"

She sipped once more. "No. Now will you sit here please, and let me share my plans with you. I want to do some cosmetic changes to this house. It is too dated, and gloomy. I want light…can we afford it?"

Rand drained his glass, and set it on the tray. "Fine. We'll start there. It needs to be done. It will double in value if you decide to sell soon. Let me see what you have here."

He sat beside her on the plush sofa and again his scent tugged at her. She was not usually aware of anything about men but after-shave and cologne that was noticeable, or lingering tobacco on most men; this was different. But this was subtle, and she liked it. It was warm, and fresh, like maybe soap, or…she blinked and opened the planner.

He took the planner from her and began to read. "You want some beautiful changes. Will you do the work? No. We'll get our contractors on it. There are a number of people who depend upon us for work…I am glad to see you will keep the furnishings. Now, here's where we will begin." He named a contractor who could oversee everything she needed.

Sondra listened to his outline and was stunned that he understood so much about what she was doing. He was going to keep it impersonal…would she want to have new linens in her mother's room? The frilly curtains and spread wouldn't sell well. And some of the artifacts were inexpensive trinkets from China, obviously…they could be disposed of, or she could pack them up for storage….

"There's a crib in her room, which was yours, so you may want to store it for further use with your children. The little nursery rhyme plaques are originals designed for Caleb just for your room, and now worth a great deal. You can deal with them however you see fit. I believe everything else of hers is in the trunks in the attic. You'll want to look into those, I imagine. Sue Lee inspected them regularly, to make certain they were not deteriorating."

"That's a lot of information in a short time, Rand Everts. How do you know all of this?"

"Caleb was thorough. He wanted everything perfect for you. And he saw to it that I was informed so that I could transfer everything to you when you came…if he was gone."

When she offered no further comment he changed the subject. "I'll call the contractor and have him make an appointment with you."

"Thank you. I appreciate that."

"I believe Her Honor, Judge Powell, will be here in a day or two. You'll want to spend some time with her, I'm sure. So, at least allow me tomorrow for introducing your inheritance? You have to know what's at stake here before you sign away a vast industry."

"I was told she would be here this week…All right, I'll let you have your way, but I doubt it will change my mind. Moreover, I want to meet this contractor and make sure I can trust him. I definitely do not want anything damaged...I need to know how he works."

"Yes, of course. Gary Topple is a General Contractor. He is independent and runs a tight ship overseeing all the work. He's rough looking, shrewd as well as biddable. He'll do a good job in here. And yes, he is insured,"

"Insurance won't replace the valuables in this house—oh, yes, I know the value of every item in every square inch. I've no intention of exposing them to reckless painters. I intend to keep artifacts and rugs, maybe just shift some things around."

He turned a page, she had written: *Does the jade really exist?*

Rand frowned, "You knew about...it wasn't a myth. He once said he regretted accepting anything from him, but the Mandarin thrust it at him, and left. There had been no opportunity to return it. Your mother feared it...he took care of it. If you are not going to take over, you won't need to concern yourself with it."

"You should give it to Sue Lee. It is her heritage."

Rand thought a moment, "Sue Lee, like most people, believes it to be a legend with no merit. Try to put it out of your mind. Caleb had his reasons for denying its existence."

Sondra shrugged, "Very well. If you are finished with my planner, I'll go up to bed. I imagine tomorrow will be quite a day."

Rand stood up, gave her his hand and helped her up off the soft cushioned couch. He handed her the planner, "Tomorrow, then. I'll see you at breakfast."

He gazed after her, and he still hadn't moved when he could hear her running up the stairs. He shook his head and sighed. And wondered at the lingering touch of her hand in his.

Bedlam reigned the next day and on into the week. The phone rang, the doorbell rang, deliveries were directed around to the kitchen for easy access, and Alma and Merilee were moving in. Millicent seemed to be having a wonderful time organizing the household. Callers appeared at the door for all sorts of services...the word was out, Powell Mansion was under assault.

Sondra interviewed Gary Topple when he came on Thursday. She was glad to escape Rand who was unrelenting with the orientation and kept her in the library for hours each day. Every new revelation about Powell Imports was unnerving. She sometimes wanted to run away from it all, but as she heard what the dire results would be if she let the company die, she found herself making decisions that she did not want to make. It was like being snared in a net, she thought, except that focusing on changing that house was sanctuary for the moment. Lurking in the future was another mansion in San Francisco…and the company headquarters—and that jade.

Gary Topple arrived just after she had spent all morning with an architect, drawing up the breakfast nook plans. He'd had some good advice, and was able to sketch quickly what he thought would work there. She could have her 5 Lite Bow Window easily. It was an excellent idea, and he would have the blueprint for her by Monday. He agreed that the kitchen was fine otherwise, and new appliances would be in order, since they had already been replaced once with the dark outdated ones, and redesigning the kitchen would not be necessary.

Merilee opened the door to Gary Toppel, and took him to the library. Sondra did not keep him waiting, and after a successful morning with the architect she had high expectations. But, the two got off to a bad start. "Gary Topple," he said. "Rand Everts said you want to make over the place so I can do everything you want done, ma'am."

Sondra frowned, "That sounds like you plan to renovate this house."

"Well, same as. He said you want outside and inside…you'll have to store the furniture, or sell it if you are gonna bring in your own stuff and live here when I'm done. And I assure you I can get siding and trim for outside at a discount. "

"Mr. Toppel, let's get things straight. I will let you know in detail what I plan to do here. I understand you do a good job; however, I am the interior decorator here and it will be done as I want it done or we have no contract."

He looked startled, shifted in the chair and said, "I, well that's unusual. An owner who is professional enough to do over a place like this. These old places do all right with a good painting and that means getting rid of all this paneling." He gestured toward the wall of bookcases. "That in itself is a beast. All those books have to come out—"

"You weren't listening, were you? Now if you can let me make the decisions I'll take you room to room and show you what *I* want *you* to do. Then you can provide me an estimate and we will go from there."

Now she took a good look at him. His bristly red hair was parted on the right side and his barber had created thick sideburns in front of his ears. His eyebrows were shaggy blonde above deep-set blue eyes. At the moment his lips were a straight line beneath high cheek bones. *This is one stubborn man.*

Sondra's gaze dropped to his plaid shirt and jeans and the turquoise ring on his left hand. She was to learn that he kept the left hand riding on his jeans pocket most of the time, while the right hand brushed at the lock of hair that persisted in falling to his forehead. Okay, she thought, and then she looked down at his feet. His feet were encased in Kevin Cole Chelsea boots.

"You make good money." She said

"Sure do. Never had anyone fuss about my work. Got some good references; for one, that Randall Everts. He has trusted me to take care of several friends of his. Says this place is to be done over, and maybe one out in 'Frisco. All you have to do is tell me what you want, and I can get it done. I guarantee my work, Ms. Powell."

"Do you have an interior decorating license? What would you do, strip the library."

"No license for that…depends on what you want. Tear out the paneling, which means taking down the book shelves and paint the walls using today's popular colors. Probably paint the shelves and put em back if you are intending to keep all those books."

"I can see," Sondra avowed, "that you and I are not going to get along at all. For your information, all I want in that library is for that only window— *that* window will be enlarged, floor to ceiling. That room needs light."

He uncrossed his legs, and whistled. "Got to have approval and permits to change the structure, ma'am."

"That is being done at this moment. There is one other change in structure, a 5 Lite Bow Window in the kitchen." Sondra stood up, wanting to dismiss him, but held her peace. He just might catch on if she was patient.

He stood up, "Let's take a look at all this stuff you want done. I'll need to make a list so I can give you an estimate…."

"I have a list of the work I want done, Mr. Toppel. I'll see you get a copy on the way out if you decide to work for me." She was striding toward the door.

What a woman, he thought. Full of surprises. Life with her would be one hell-of-a merry ground. Our kids would toe the mark…

He tilted his red head, his blue eyes were twinkling, as his body finally calmed down—not his mind—after she disappeared from view.

Gary Toppel sprinted to the door, needing to catch up to her.

"Another Caleb Powell. Do this. Do that. Ah well…." He murmured.

Chapter Eight

Sondra was in the library in the process of removing the ancient blue velvet drapery from the small, double-hung window, which had been lost behind the bulk and appeared never to have been opened. The cloth was faded, streaked with original blue in the folds, and dust flew, giving her a mustache. She was unaware of it and the streak of dust across her cheek. She sneezed a couple of times, folded the panels as carefully as possible and slipped everything into a bag provided by the dry-cleaner. The bag would be picked up in the afternoon, and when the drapes had been cleaned she would decide a use for them.

"If the fabric isn't rotten, it will still have some purpose, I believe," she murmured and sealed the bag. "I am definitely going to have a big window with drapes that will open or tie back. Depends on the cloth I choose."

She heard the doorbell and female voices immediately followed by a little scream of delight. Merilee was declaring, "Miss Sue Lee. Judge Powell! How good to see you again. You didn't have to ring…you have a key. So come in—you didn't bring luggage; you aren't staying?"

"Hello, dear Merilee. No luggage. I'm staying at the apartment. It is closer to the court. And I have a full week there. So, is she here? Rand said she has arrived. Will she want to see me? Do you know? I have waited so long for this." She set her black Chanel handbag on the foyer table beside the familiar jade figurine, and went inside, unaware of Merilee's astonishment at casual treatment of something as pricy as that bag. Merilee followed with a sigh.

Sondra felt a moment of panic. She stood holding that dry-cleaning bag, she was covered in dust, dressed in wrinkled cargo pants and a red tee shirt.

Definitely not the sort of clothes to meet *her*...the Judge. Exactly who is she? Millicent said Caleb adopted her... Escape was impossible as Merilee and a formidable figure filled the doorway. *Is she my sister?*

"Sondra, here's Judge Powell to see you. I think this is so exciting. It has been so long since you were together."

Anyone observing this reunion would have noticed that, except for Sue Lee's darker silken hair and slightly almond shaped grey eyes in contrast to Sondra's fairness, they were same height, and nearly the same weight; but there it ended.

A professional, Sue Lee never dressed casually. She was too much in the limelight, it was not a thing she had learned in Gem's care. Thus, she wore suits especially designed for her in subdued colors and fine fabrics. Today she had chosen a green boucle knit that was so dark as to appear black. Her blouse could have been the lining of an oyster shell, silky and creamy, and her only ornament was a pendant of green jade on a gold chain. Embedded in the jade was the gold Chinese Zodiac symbol of resolution, which was the symbol of an April-May birth. It had been her graduation gift from Gem who had discovered her birth date in the documents provided by her Mandarin father when she took over the care of this child.

"Sondra?" Sue Lee moved tentatively into the room. "I am so pleased to see you. But so sad that it is for the reason of loss. Caleb will be missed by many people. He was good to me. And he was so lonely for you all those years. He was generous, never wanting to take you away from your aunt and break her heart. He always said that the two of you were among friends who would take good care of you. But I knew he yearned for you to be here with him."

Sondra set the cleaner's bag aside and tried to gather her thoughts. Her mind was betraying her with memory of a little girl who held her and crooned words she couldn't understand. Words that were endearments in a strange language. She brushed at her dusty clothes, "Judge Powell, you will have to forgive me. I don't usually welcome visitors in such a state. Please have a seat and I'll ask Merilee to bring us some refreshment."

Sue Lee gazed at her, seeing the resentment that Rand had told her about. "Please, won't you call me Sue Lee...You have a daunting task ahead. Rand tells me you are going to liven this place up. Caleb would not let us do a thing but keep it clean in the years I grew up here. I'll be glad to see it restored."

"I don't think it was the most cheerful place for a child," Sondy offered. "I wouldn't know, since I was so small when he gave me away."

Sue Lee flinched. Rand had reason to be concerned. She looked for the nearest chair, "I'll sit here, thank you. I won't keep you long since you didn't expect me, and since I have an appearance in court at three o'clock. I was so eager to see you again, I couldn't wait to come—forgive this intrusion."

"Intrusion? This is your home, more so than mine. I am the intruder." Merilee was still in the doorway. "Merilee could you bring a tray of refreshments, please. I think you will know what to get for Miss Powell...you and your mother come, too. I know that you are all long-time friends."

"Oh, no, Sondy, mom and I are baking for tonight's dinner and a few days ahead. You two will do fine...I'll be right back...."

"Well, so..." Sondy gestured, "I seem to have created a dusty room with the removal of those drapes. Perhaps Rand told you what I am doing to the house...that will be a floor to ceiling window when I'm through. A reading room should have light. And there will be new drapes that will open and close...no longer these heavy things that hung there forever."

This is a safe subject, thought Sue Lee. But she said, "The only time I was in here for any length of time was when Caleb spent a day with us and he would read to me from the children's books on that shelf. I was usually in the nursery, then my own room when Gem didn't have some place for us to go when school was out and on weekends. She was a fun person to live with. We did a lot of things together."

She sat forward on her chair, "It took me a while to relax with our visits to Chinatown and her people—my people? Our language was difficult because of some differences...but I was learning English, too, and most of the people there spoke only Chinese...it was a confusing mess for a great while. When I was older, I could sort it out, finally."

Merilee interrupted with a tray of tea and little sandwiches and pastries. She left it on the desk and Sue Lee automatically rose and went to pour the tea. "Do you take sugar and cream or lemon?" She turned to look at Sondy and realized her mistake immediately.

"I'm so sorry. Forgive me. It was so familiar...I used to do this...Oh, Sondra. I did not mean to hurt you!"

"Why would you think I am hurt? This is your home."

"No, no it isn't. Not anymore. It is yours. Your father amassed a fortune for you. I have not wanted anything more from him. He was kind to me, but

Gem was my parent and they never let me forget my dual heritage. I have lived with it, and finally decided to be who I am and devil take the hindmost!" Fortified, she said, "So, sit still in your disheveled state and let me serve us some tea. We'll get our prospective right in a moment. Now, sugar or lemon?"

Sondy felt herself relax slightly. "Lemon, please."

The mansion make-over was the safe topic of conversation until they had exhausted the subject. They sipped, ate little sandwiches and finally returned cups and plates to the tray. Sue Lee turned to her, "I want desperately to hug you. I have been your sister all my life, and would love to continue in that vein. You were really all I had when your mom died. A sister somewhere in the world who had been taken away from me. Oh, I did realize, eventually, that Caleb separated us because of the culture differences. He *did not* want you to learn Chinese ways from me...how I would have loved growing up with you. But it was not to be."

"You won't want to hug me right now. I am covered with dust..."

"I can't wait," said Sue Lee as she got up and went to Sondra, and she threw her arms around Sondra and held her, and held her still, as Sondra returned the embrace.

The years melted away and Sondra was the toddler and Sue Lee was the child. How could she, she wondered, have thought this person had taken her place in the family? Her frostiness began to melt as they separated and stood holding hands, the years passing before them but bringing them together again. "Oh, Sue Lee," she whispered.

"Won't you come stay here with us?" Sondra asked.

"I have an apartment close to the court...and James is with me. We are to be married in June, so it's all right for us to share the place. I don't want to be in the way of the work you plan to do. But I love what Rand said you are doing...it is a dark and gloomy place. I'll see you when I have free time, if that's okay? And now, shouldn't I be meeting your Aunt? She was very special to mother you all these years. I remember her kindness to me—do you think she remembers me?"

They had been unaware that Millicent stood in the doorway, tearing up as she gazed at the two young women. No longer able to remain silent, "Beautiful Willow," she cried, "they told me you were here. A grown woman, now, and successful. As are both of you. Sondy is owner of a successful Interior Design Shop—"

"Miss Millie," Sue Lee held her hands out to Millicent. "You remember me? Yes that is the meaning of my Chinese name… I was only nine years old when you went away." They clasped hands and then went into a brief hug.

"I'd know you anywhere, my dear. You are even lovelier now. Caleb was wise in his decisions, I can see that now. Neither of you had a father figure to care for you, but obviously he was in the background and saw that you both had the care to develop you potential. Come, have a seat and tell us about your life which has led you to practice law."

"You know, ma'am, this is how I remembered you, always well-groomed, wearing your lovely skirts and sweaters, walking shoes that carried us out for trips to that place for ice cream…and I told Gem many times that we must always wear some jewelry like Miss Millie. And she laughed at me, but we did it, and one time Caleb came to see us and remarked that we were as bad as his sister for the jewelry." She waited for their laughter to subside, then added, "I didn't decide right away to go into law. But several families in Chinatown were the victims of a prejudiced attorney, and I swore one day to do something about it. I told Caleb, and he was able to get them some justice after all, and from there it was always the law for me.

The reunion between Sue Lee and Millicent was much warmer than between the two girls at first. Millicent got herself a plate and cup of tea, and the past was filled in as far as they could go in the next hour. So much to share…twenty years to fill in. However, no one mentioned the jade at that first meeting.

Sue Lee took her leave reluctantly, but allowing herself half an hour to get to the courthouse and her meeting, she collected her purse, took out her cellular phone and called James. "Hey boy, I am ready to go to work. Come get me…of course I do love you. How else could I be so familiar with you?" She laughed and snapped the device closed.

"Will we meet him, your James—soon?" Millicent probed.

Sondra gasped, "Sue Lee, the two of you must come for dinner. We would love it. Can you get away for that? We dine about seven o'clock."

"That would be too much trouble for you…we can grab a pizza…"

"No, of course not," Sondra argued. "Rand will be here with us, and Rafe Barker will be coming…I have hired a contractor named Toppel and he will join us tonight…Please say yes."

"You really must come, dear Sue Lee. And bring James. We will want to be invited to the wedding and it will help to get acquainted ahead of that event. You may need our advice regarding James," Millicent urged.

Sue Lee laughed, "All right, you two. It will be good to see Rafe again. James won't like it, but—"

"James doesn't like Rafe? Goodness," groaned Millicent. "Why ever not? Have they had some trouble?"

"I...I dated Rafe a couple of times. Before I was engaged. James thinks we are in love. But we never were. It was just friendship coming at a difficult time for me...James will be fine. I will tell him the wedding is off if he doesn't have his head on straight." She rolled her eyes and stared at the ceiling for a moment. "Hey, you really do need to clean up this house. Look—that stain up there was done by one of my teenage friends who learned that if you shake certain beverages they will, uh, they will hit the ceiling."

Sondra laughed, Millie said, "Goodness," as she looked up at the stain, and then she too laughed. On that note they saw Sue Lee out the door and into the Black Nissan sedan that came for her. They were not able to get a good look at James, but he did fill up the driver space.

As they watched the car speed away, Millicent murmured, "My. What a day this was."

Sondra went immediately to talk to Alma. "I've done a terrible thing to you. I have invited Sue Lee and James, and Gary Toppel and Rafe Baxter to dinner tonight. With the five of us can we handle that many guests on this short notice?"

"Oh, honey don't you worry about a thing. I have a standing rib that will feed an army. Merilee and I will not sit down to eat—no, now we can't do that all the time. We need to have our meal earlier, so we don't get too tired. That works better for us...now is this menu good for you?" She pointed to the blackboard and Sondra smiled.

"Everything good, Alma. What a wonder you are in the kitchen. I am sure glad to see the asparagus...I love it."

"And looks like you found some love from the past, too. She is a good woman. She has had much to endure...being mixed race doesn't always set with a lot of people and they don't make any bones about letting you know. Don't even blink an eye, they just walk away from knowing some of the finest people in the world...oops, there's my buzzer, got to finish the rolls and loaves of bread now, so every things a-go here. Better get a shower now, or do plan to be the dirty faced kid at the table tonight."

"Oh, you. Alma Watson. Of course I will. And just so you know, the bag in the library is for the dry cleaner...not the garbage. Okay?"

"You sending a bag of dust to be dry cleaned?"

"Alma! No, that's the drapes from over the window."

"What window? In the library? Oh, I remember. There is one there...."

"Exit laughing," murmured Sondra, as she went to shower.

Six people in best dress were in the old parlor at seven o'clock when Alma called them to dinner. If anyone noticed the dimness in the dining room, no one remarked. They were all busy getting acquainted around the oval mahogany table which allowed one to visit without having to talk across ones neighbor. A necessary evil, Sondra thought, if they were to work together to put things in order.

She had decided, in the shower, that she *would* travel to San Francisco, to Powell House, and begin renovation at once. She would spend whatever time it took to complete the task then she could go home with a sense of satisfaction. Especially when she deeded over one of the houses to Sue Lee and James as a wedding present.

As for the rest of the estate, she would do what was necessary to save Powell Imports. Rafe would surely guide her as she took over, and in a short while she could place everything into the hands of a new owner, Rand Everts. She would give him ownership and not look back.

Feeling satisfied at her decisions, Sondra enjoyed the dinner beside Gary Toppel who was just as comfortable in his suit and tie as he had been in jeans. "I ordered the paint you wanted today. Should be here in time to start maybe Saturday. That work for you, Miss Powell."

"Are your painters careful, Mr. Toppel? Will they move the furnishings around with no damage? Are they to be depended upon to come and go at the same time every day?"

"Not to worry. Plan to do most of it myself. We brush-paint for a job like this. Even though we cover everything, I don't like to be messy. I have a guy who is a vet, only things is he sometimes has to be away for therapy on his prosthesis...he lost a leg in the Middle East. Great guy and dependable. I enjoy working beside him on special jobs. He's a baritone and sings his heart out while he lays down paint...you'll like him, I'm sure."

"I plan to," Sondra said, as she sipped her wine. She gazed around the table and locked gazes with Rand Everts whose eyes were all that smiled at her.

Chapter Nine

Beside her on the left, James Kwan said, "What will you do to the place, Miss Powell? Sue Lee tells me you want to brighten it up." He smoothed his light blue silk tie with long slender fingers; in the same manner as the other men present, he'd removed the jacket of his navy blue suit, and had folded up his white shirt cuffs. James, a first generation American, was a tall man, as one could expect since his father was from the North Provinces of China where they are taller, and his American mother's two brothers were men who dealt with height daily.

"James' mother," explained Sue Lee, "was a news correspondent to China where she met his father, Shen Kwan. They defied prejudice, settled in New York, and raised their son whose family name, Kwan, translated means 'to concern or to involve'."

"True to his name, and as an International Attorney, he became an advocate of the deprived. Now, with genuine interest he added, "Interior decorating must be a lot of work."

Sondra replied, "Yes, I love the work—but, for goodness sake, don't be so formal. I am Sondra…I'm doing some cosmetic touches, James. Paint, new fabrics in some instances. I'll switch some of the beautiful rugs to places compatible with the colors I will use. They are old and valuable so I don't want to lose them."

"How about the house in 'Frisco? It is Queen Ann Victorian, not like this mansion."

"I haven't been there yet. Not sure what it needs. I understand that Caleb lived there, so he may not have neglected it like he did this one."

"You are angry about this? You seem to resent something..."

"I don't *want* any of this. Caleb was nothing to me. It is taking me away from a prosperous business..."

"Leave her alone, James." Sue Lee advised. "She has a big load to bear right now. She needs to come to terms on her own...so, Sondy, I have something to ask of you. It's about the wedding dresses in the attic. There are two of them. I would love to wear one for my wedding if that is agreeable to you."

"I haven't even been up there. Two gowns? I wonder whose they were. When can you come? We can go up together and look at them."

"I could probably make it Saturday...I love them both, but one was your mother's and I would not want to take that one. You will want it for your wedding, I am sure."

Such a thing had never occurred to Sondra. She sat quietly, until someone asked her a question and she was back in the room. *My mother's wedding dress as Millie described it?*

Gary Toppel said, "What do you want me to do about the *gee-gaws* in the dining room? I can have a packer come and get them put away before we start..."

He called the china gee-gaws?

Rafe spoke from across the table and conversation picked up as the plates were removed, desert arrived, and more wine was poured. "Sondra, I understand," Rafe affirmed, "that you will be coming in to the office on Tuesday to sign the papers and take over Powell Imports. If that is the case, we need to have some of the department heads there, and reporters...I'll have it all set up for say two o'clock?" Every voice was stilled instantly.

Sondra looked at him, but all she could see was her life being changed. With a shake of her head, she murmured, "I don't want this! Can't it be done without fanfare? Why involve the media? It doesn't need to go to all the world, does it?"

Rand said, "Sondra, if we don't do it this way, giving out the information we want them to have, you will have reporters all over the place and the conjecture and speculation about you will be bad publicity for Power Imports. And you. You can do this. I will be at your side, making the announcement. All you have to do is give the prepared statement of acceptance and it's over."

Like someone lost underground, Sondra looked at Millicent who nodded so slightly that only Sondra saw it. She sighed. "Tomorrow I must attend Caleb Powell's Memorial Service, and Tuesday I must assume his life." She stared at Rand "Will I ever get my own back?"

No one commented for a moment. "Seems to me like you will have it all, Miss Powell," Gary Toppel offered, turning his wine glass on the white tablecloth. "Think now, you can do your interior decorating while the import business with Rand as CEO goes on as usual. How would that be, I ask you."

Sondra stared at him, gazed around the table and saw the compassion in every face. "Don't pity me!" she exclaimed. "I am not afraid of responsibility. I have training that will help me through it all, as well as the company executives doing their own jobs. What I don't like is the assumption all around that I appreciate what Caleb Powell has done—leaving me such a legacy. Hear me now, once and for all. I do not claim him as my father...he wasn't, in a true sense. I hardly even know what he looked like...try to understand."

The silence was all she needed, "Just be the true friends I will require for the next months and do not judge my decisions. If they are not good, be kind enough to discuss it with me. I need you—all of you."

Sue Lee got up and came to Sondra, "Darling Sondy. We are here. We are going all the way with you. Wherever that leads us." She pulled her up into her arms. There was stir, audible sighs of relief and then someone began the conversation about the discovery of the window in the library, and the evening continued uneventfully.

One by one the guests took their leave. Sue Lee and James promised to visit again on the weekend. "We'll see you at the memorial tomorrow," James affirmed, as they went out into the night. Gary Toppel moved in close to Sondra, he took her hand and held onto it. "One gutsy woman, love. Pleasure to work for you. See you later." She could not help following his exit with her gaze. *I have a problem...he's too much like Bradley...*

Rafe hung back, obviously hoping to have her alone, but Rand remained at her side; all Rafe could do was hug Millicent and take Sondra's hand for a moment. "We'll need to leave about ten thirty in the morning. The service is at eleven. It's being held in the PTS Memorial Center which he built for returning servicemen and women; the chapel is huge enough to accommodate the crowd wanting to pay last respects."

"The company limo will be here, Rafe," Rand asserted. "We'll all go in it. Bishop Sandhurst will ride with us. I know, we'll have to see to his return, too. But I will want to bring Millicent and Sondra directly home. He won't want to linger because he is a busy man."

"What about Sue Lee and James. Will we have room for them?"

Rand looked uneasy for a moment, "Her Honor will be in a second limo with company exec's…that's what she wants. I couldn't talk her out of it." He ran his palms over his temples and hair, showing fatigue for a second. "James will stay with her…they'll come to the house afterward. Not much more to say, it's all planned. I've taken care of everything."

Millicent cried, "That is *not* right. She is the adopted daughter of Caleb Powell."

"That was her request, Mrs. Sherman. She wants to avoid publicity."

Sondra stared at him, "Rand. Is there more to this? What would they have to say about her? She is legally a Powell…."

"And well known on her own merit. Her story would open a lot of questions…her father came to an awful end in the hands of the Communists. The story of his having a child somewhere in America was foremost in the papers for some time." He unclenched his fist. "Caleb kept her protected—he did a hell of a job of that. So, if that's all, Rafe, we'll see you here in the morning. Undoubtedly it will be a grueling day. Then one more day out in San Francisco and it will settle down, I am sure."

"Are you really, Rand? I wonder if they are going to let me alone."

"Not for a few weeks, Sondy. You will make the news every time they can get a news story. But it will end. We just have to endure it. Or they will turn on you, the bad ones, that is."

Rafe gripped her arm, "Good night then. See you ladies tomorrow." And he was gone out the door, and perhaps out of mind as Millicent excused herself and went to her rooms.

The room was quiet as they stood looking at each other. Rand spoke first, "You'd best get some rest, Sondy."

"I just realized the enormity of your responsibilities in this, this…situation. You had it all done before I got here, didn't you?"

He winced, "Sondra, we are looking at a chapel that holds fifteen hundred people. I had it reserved. It began the day he died, Sondy. I was the only one to do it…of all the people Caleb Powell helped in his lifetime, I was the one he trusted to do my job and do it well."

"This was part of your job?"

"No, not really. He knew that I came to—maybe love is too strong—to respect and admire him more than my own father. But that's another story. I am so glad that you will be there, with me. It is what he wanted. I have arranged a private viewing for you… a couple of minutes after you appear in the chapel."

She moaned. "No, no. I can't. Rand, please…" She put her hands on his chest and felt his heartbeat. Looking up, the dark eyes were even darker as he put his arms around her, carefully.

"You can do it, Sondra. I'll help you. Trust me." And then he said a surprising thing, "Do you believe in God, Sondy? Did Millicent see to your religious education? Fine then. We will do this together." He kissed her on the temple, next to her eye. "Goodnight, Miss Powell. If you find yourself unable to trust me, try God. He is much more powerful than I am."

It was after one o'clock before Sondra felt the burden lessen, and got herself into bed. It was an hour later when she saw the clock for the last time, and she slept. But surprisingly she did not dream of funerals, she dreamed of being kissed on the temples of her face…their pulses had throbbed together for an instant…now the dream was a pounding drum. She gasped and woke up. In the dimness of night, she lay wondering what that was all about. "It was just a friendly kiss…nothing more," she whispered into the silence, and turned over and went back to further dreamless sleep.

The kitchen was empty when Sondra went down to breakfast. But there was coffee, tea and toast available and she got out some cheddar cheese, cut a couple of slices for her toast, and melted it in the toaster oven. She found a bowl of cut fruit in the refrigerator and placed a couple of pieces of cantaloupe on her plate, took out the melted cheese-toast and with her cup of coffee went to the library. Millicent was on her way down the stairs, grumbling.

"Morning, Sondy. My stomach is being delicate this morning, so, earlier, I had a little yogurt with berries…that toast looks enticing, but not yet—I have always liked that outfit. It is professional looking and it becomes you, dear. Is that Navy blue? Yes, I thought so. The print tunic is in style, although I for one am not too fond of handkerchief hems."

"I didn't know you had a black suit, Millie. When did you get that one? It isn't going to be too warm, is it?"

"Oh, no. It is not wool…they can be hot. I bought this for Wallace's…you know. I think they said it is silk…so I'll be fine in this." She finished her coffee and set the cup into the saucer. "Rand left a few minutes ago. He went to the office here in Sacramento and said he would be back with a Limousine…I do dread this Sondy. But, that's life, I guess. Once it's done we won't have it to do again."

Sondra bit into her toast and savored the melted cheese. "That's a blessing. Heaven only knows what this is going to be like. I've no idea how many people will be there."

"I believe you had best be prepared for a very large crowd, honey."

Rafe arrived shortly after they had eaten. Alma and Merilee had put in an appearance in somber apparel, and it was not long before Rand let himself in and met them in the library. "I took the liberty of getting Bishop Sandhurst over to the chapel. He wanted to see to things."

Totally unaware of his good looks in a light gray suit, he said, "Everyone ready? Good. We need to get going. Traffic is heavy and may delay us…we'll be ready for lunch right after the memorial, so reservations are made for two o'clock at Top Of The Town in the hotel building. I think we will have the best privacy there. After the service and crowds I was sure you would not want more confusion to deal with during lunch." He gestured, "So, shall we go? Our driver is waiting."

The Limo accommodated all of them. Rand seated himself beside Sondra and took her hand as they eased out onto the street. "It will be all right, Sondy," he murmured softly.

Sondra had only seen such events on television, or occasionally for some dignitary who was being honored in New York. The chapel was fortunately located in an easy-to-access place. The traffic was slow, the lines endless. As they stopped before an immense Italianate style building, she noted the grounds and what appeared to be an overflow of potted plants in the entryway.

Rand gave her a hand out of the car, kept her close with his hand on her back, and seemed to her to be preventing Rafe from getting close. But Rafe was being protective of Millie and they made their way inside, down the aisle of a formidable room with balcony to the front seats. And from there it seemed that the world quietly filtered in and took up all the seats in the building. There was a sniff, someone coughed, and whispers were soft and unintelligible. She was gazing around at thousands of people in a haze when Rand said, "Come with me, both of you."

Both women stood up. They followed Rand to a door behind the lectern. When he opened the door of the darkly draped room, the wood casket on its stand with the lid up was waiting for them. The attendant stepped aside. "Madam, Miss Powell…." He gestured to the casket which Sondra later learned, when she saw the expense sheet, was oak veneer with almond satin lining.

"Caleb!" Millicent dashed to the side; she placed her gloved hand on Caleb's head, "Oh, brother, you got so white-headed. But God will know you. And Susan is waiting no longer. The two of you are together." She put her head down on his chest, spilling tears on his hands and sobbing uncontrollably.

Sondra put her arms around her aunt and looked down into the serene face of Caleb Powell. "So that's who you are…You never gave me a chance to love you. How am I to grieve for you—someone I never knew," she whispered. She felt a hand on her back and looked up.

Rand was offering the only comfort he could with that touch. It was genuine, as was his look of sorrow at the loss of his friend. "You will get to know him soon." He murmured.

Not like this. Not here, Sondra thought and patiently waited. Presently she spoke.

"Let's go, Millie. The service is ready to begin. They need to close this and move it out to the chapel. We have seen him, now. Come." Sondra urged her back to their seats in the overflowing chapel, the music began and the hour passed as she observed the Bishop's faultless presentation of the Memorial Service. She held Millie's hand on one side, and Rand held hers on the other. Still Sondra Powell felt nothing for Caleb, her father.

She grew restless at the eulogies from so many people; she was saved by the solo of a baritone whose voice filled the room, and surely was strong enough to boost Caleb's spirit directly to heaven. A children's choir raised their young voices in two unfamiliar hymns. It was then that Sondra looked at the front seats to her right and saw Sue Lee and James, and a woman in a silk print dress. Her almond eyes and fair complexion named her without introduction. Gem Chang had come to pay her respects, or to support Sue Lee? Sue Lee said something to her, and she turned to meet Sondra's gaze. She nodded ever so slightly.

Sondra sighed. She looked back at Millicent who was suddenly pale. "Millie, are you all right?"

Millie whispered shakily, "I should have made him—"

She slumped against Sondra. Rand reached over and touched her, he moved swiftly to lift Millie up in his arms and make a quick exit, again into the viewing room. Sondra forgot where she was, she followed along, noticing a couple who dashed in behind them pulling the door closed Thinking it was the press, she began to protest when the man said, "Miss Powell, I am a doctor. This is my wife…I thought she got pale pretty fast. Caleb's sister, right? Put her here on this couch, get me a pillow, Mavis honey, over there on the table…"

To Sondra, he said, "I am—was Caleb's doctor."

Mavis handed him a vial from her handbag. Declaring Millicent had fainted, he used the vial and she stirred at last.

"You are okay, Mrs. Sherman. I'm Doctor Bergman, Caleb's physician. You fainted, that's all right. It's not every day that two thousand people gather in one place. But not surprising. Caleb Powell was an extraordinary man of his generation and beyond."

Millicent sat up slowly, "Thank you. I'm fine now. We need to go back inside."

"It isn't necessary, Mrs. Sherman." The doctor was checking her pulse once more.

"I have something to say to them."

"Very well, Rand can you give her a hand?" Still in charge he said, "Here's the Bishop. She would like to address the mourners…is that possible Andrew"?

"Yes, of course." Bishop Sandhurst murmured, "They'll be happy to know that she's fine. Take my arm Millicent. I'll accompany you to the lectern. You'll be able to hang on to that if you feel the need for support."

"That is kind of you, Bishop Sandhurst." She took his arm and gave him a radiant smile.

The room filled with gentle applause as Millie took the stand. Sondra remained beside her. And Rand continued to stay beside her with his hand on her back.

"I am sure," Millicent opened, "you are aware that I am Caleb Powell's sister. Thank you for coming. The enormous crowd here this morning is uplifting—as was the service for Caleb. I imagine you are wondering what happens next. Sondra Gaye Powell, his daughter, has accepted the legacy, and the company will continue as is. Again, thank you for bidding our father and brother a most auspicious farewell, shepherded by Bishop Sandhurst."

The applause was deafening. Sondra looked at Rand and let him see her pain and he knew it was for what she was giving up. He searched out her hand, gave her a gentle squeeze and said,

"This ends it for now, Sondra. You can check out the final resting place at any time you wish. Ah, here's Sue Lee and James, let's go. It's time to go."

Chapter Ten

The press release of the memorial was handled without sensationalism, simply because Rand had intervened. He had scheduled a press session the morning before at the Sacramento office of Powell Imports conference room and provided pictures for release. At that time he let them know that when the transfer of ownership was complete, there would be occasion in San Francisco for them to address Miss Powell directly. Until then, he suggested they give her time to recover from the stress of such events. Yes, he could assure them that in future, the company would be holding regular press conferences. Advance notices would go out in a timely manner.

To prove the company's goodwill, he invited the reporters to be their guests for lunch in the cafeteria on the first floor. He watched them file out. It would be honest reporting in the days ahead. News of Caleb Powell's death would reverberate around the world, and Millie and Sondy would be treated kindly.

Even though the days after the service were spent quietly at home, it took Millie a couple of those days to regain her color and energy. The press had been sparing of details regarding her statement, and the fainting spell; nevertheless, some speculation did crop up about Sondra Powell's takeover of Powell Imports. Ignoring the nay-sayers, Rand was convinced that Sondra had the capability of doing it just as Caleb had expected.

Still, when faced with his own feelings he was unable to admit that he was attracted to her and felt a need to be special to her. He told himself that she surely *did not* need that sort of complication in her life right now; an affair was the last thing she needed to challenge her vulnerability further. Thoroughly self-chastised, he returned to San Francisco, with every intention of coming back for her...after he regained his senses. If he could.

A week after the service, Sondra finally got out the briefcase with all the paperwork that had been supplied by the attorney and the head of the company. There were not a few documents, there were books of them and, astonishingly they did not duplicate any information; what she was continuing to learn amazed her even more. Only once did she question Millie, saying, "Do you know the exact number of holdings in this estate? Have you any idea of the laws, requirements—and there are bills of lading, licenses, duties, customs in export, and even airways are sometimes involved, Aunt Millie? To say nothing of agreements and meeting schedules..."

"I only know that it is vast, my dear. I always said Caleb had a silver spoon in his mouth when he was born. He was a shrewd businessman, but fair in his dealings, and compassionate with those less fortunate, which makes the difference in a successful life and a failed one."

Sondra stared at her. *Compassion didn't pay our bills.* "You consider him successful? In all things?" She picked up a sheaf of papers. "This is a proposal before the board, which has been tabled because of the...they want to add Export to our title. It looks well prepared, but think, Millie, of the documents. It's mind-boggling!"

"My, that shows growth in the right direction...no one is perfect, Sondy. If you think he failed us, remember that it was my fault. I should have let him know...but I didn't. I can't undo that. I can only forge ahead toward my ordained destiny...whatever that may be. I can stay on with you if you like. But I can also return to our little house and be very content; although I will never be the same again, if I am separated from you."

"Whatever gave you the idea that you would be going home without me? We stay together from here on, Millicent Sherman. We go home together when I have ended this ownership in a year or so. By then I will know to whom, and how, I can transfer ownership."

Millicent raised her hand to her mouth which was open in a silent oh. "Oh, you aren't going to do that. How can you think of such a thing...I know that almost twenty thousand people are employed by Powell holdings...you see, Caleb confided that a while back. And even more people depend on us in many industries. We have trade agreements to honor, and to suddenly cut them off by giving it away—I did not raise you to think so selfishly, Sondra."

Papa's Jade

Sondra could not reply. Millicent—unusual for her—was still in her dressing gown, having come down to have coffee before starting her day. The lace trimmed peignoir was sheer pink and revealed the soft print gown beneath it. It was the only exposed clothing she ever wore.

"No. No you didn't, Darling Millie. Thank you. If I appear to be rebelling, it's because I would not have deliberately chosen such a life. I suppose I don't welcome the responsibility of thousands of people. That's too much for one person—I hope to heaven that Caleb was into electronics or we will never be caught up with document preparation—and Millie, have you noticed the number of jade artifacts he brought over from China? We probably import that stuff, too."

"Settle down, darling. You aren't a one-person shop. You are at the top of a large corporation here. You have hundreds of people working for you, and so far they have done an outstanding job. I do believe they will be loyal to you…Rand Everts is not going to let you fail. He can guide you, and you are capable of making good decisions, you know. Give it a chance, will you?" She didn't wait for an answer, but headed for the door, "Well, dear one, I had best get dressed before that Toppel man gets here. Have you seen the green he put on the dining room walls?"

"He did what?" She jumped up and sprinted for the dining room. The walls were now a bright green, and Susan saw red. She began her search, and found Toppel in the library with the carpenter as they were working at enlarging the window. All had been covered with heavy plastic covers, and they had a vacuum working to catch the sawdust. She hesitated before yelling out his name.

The noise ceased and he turned to her. "Yes ma'am?"

"You have done justice to the front entry. You followed my instructions and it is exactly as I want it to look. Fine, now the kitchen is coming along, I see your men are creating my bow window. I hope you use the paint color *which I chose* for the room as well. Now. May I ask where you got the paint you used in the dining room? And please advise me as to who it was that said it was to be painted…I ordered the wallpaper and expected it to be used. Why wasn't it? Do you have trouble following orders? If so, get yourself out of here. You no longer work for me."

"Oh, come on now—you've worked up steam—I thought it looked better than—"

"If you wish to fulfill your contract you will see to it that the wallpaper is applied immediately, that the room is finished just as I ordered. If you make another decision like that anywhere in this house, you will be sued for breach of contract. I will let this one go, because it may accept the paper without bleeding through. I just hope so. The paper I bought for that room is white with bouquets of roses and lavender ribbon streamers…you will supply the manpower to correct this at your expense. If you have a problem with that, pack up and get out. You have today to make up your mind. I will have your decision by six tonight when you are leaving for the day. Can you handle that?"

"Hey, lady, what I can't handle is your attitude in front of my employees—"

"Then you should see to it that I don't *need* to have an attitude with you because of your failure to comply with my *need* to have it done right. I know my business, the redecorating will keep to the period, and it will be lighter."

She left Gary Toppel red in the face; the carpenter instantly wiped off the surprised look on his face. She tramped through the kitchen and out onto the back porch, and sat down in a chair and opened the briefcase. She lifted out a huge thick document and began studying the agreements and financial records, and lists of contacts and contracts; she stopped trembling at last. "Terrible way to start the day," she whispered.

Within an hour she had to admit that if she stayed with this estate for the rest of her life, she would have to somehow include her SG Interior Design Company in Powell Imports, and choose an Executive Officer in order to keep it going. Of course she could sell out, but hanging on would keep them under the protection of the corporation. Surely Rand would be thrilled with the decision. *Why should I think he'd care?*

About ten thirty she went inside, called the Sacramento office, spoke with the manager, Afton Van Alt, and requested a conference with whomever was available. She'd expected a next-day accommodation, but Van Alt insisted, "We have been expecting you. We are looking forward to this time with you. Two o'clock it is. We will see you then."

She called Rafe and asked him to accompany her. He suggested lunch downtown first, since they would only be a few doors away and could get right over to the office.

"You don't have to start so soon, Sondra. But if you are ready, they can provide you with a good picture of the works up here…I'll pick you up in about an hour."

She closed her cellular phone. "No time for panic. Get dressed Sondy," she murmured.

She took time to let Millicent know where she'd be, then hurried to change into business-like attire. She chose a blue tweed look, a two piece knit dress that draped so nicely she had known it would be a favorite because of the stand-up collar, and four flat, three-inch blue buttons on the jacket. Black pumps and nine-millimeter white pearl earrings, a bag to match the shoes and she went down the stairs just as Rafe arrived.

He whistled, "Wow. You will get their attention or I miss my calling as professional admirer of beautiful women."

"Stick to your law practice, Rafe Barker. I may need you for more than a boost to my ego. Like, I may need help with Gary Toppel."

"What has he done to you, Sondra?"

"I'll tell you over lunch. It is rather complicated."

Nodding his agreement he put her into his white Oldsmobile and took off for uptown.

Sondra was distraught as they lunched lightly on seafood salad, sourdough rolls and peach sherbet. Rafe listened with a frown most of the time, but was appalled at the behavior of Rand's recommended contractor. Why would Toppel behave like that, he wondered? That guy knew the business, why was he giving Sondra the business. Must not have expected her response, probably thought she would just let him take over…well he saw the real woman this morning and it was a bet that Toppel would not try anything more. Too much money and his prestige at stake…*Good Lord is the guy trying to work up a seduction?*

"There are better ways of getting a woman's attention," he whispered to himself but she heard him.

"What are you talking about? Gary? Why would he need my attention? He has a job to do for me, that's all. Nothing more. I once knew a guy like him…and I didn't marry him. And I will not even consider being civil to that man. He painted the dining room a foul green, and then when I called him on it, did he apologize for not using the wall paper instead? No. He got mad because I called him on it in front of his employee."

"Oh. Oh." Rafe sighed. "That does not sound like Gary Toppel. But who knows what happens to some men when then see something they want really badly?"

"Have you lost your mind, Rafe Barker?"

"No, I just found it again. But here, we need to get over to your first day on the job. I know you are going to like these folks…"

He proceeded to list 'these folks' one by one as they left the restaurant and walked rapidly with the light, crossed the street and went into the Liberal Insurance Building, to the third floor and past an imposing brass sign that said:

Office of President Caleb Powell
Powell Imports Inc.
Sacramento, CA

Afton Van Alt was leaning against the receptionist's desk when they arrived a bit breathless from a meal and brisk walk. Rafe knew him personally, was always impressed with his skill as the manager of Caleb's office. He seemed to know exactly what Caleb expected and once having accomplished it, was satisfied in his suave way. All he needed to do was reach up and check out his Adolphe Menjou mustache, waxed and debonair looking, and forego gloating over his achievements.

He was not as large as Rafe. Slim and under six feet tall, he seemed almost delicate for a man. In the language of the now deceased movie star, Menjou, Afton was suave looking—debonair. Rafe knew him to be an excellent, shrewd businessman who never got a spot of anything on his light-colored suits. And there it ended, for he spent his spare time in some pretty challenging sports, was proficient in Karate, and was an opponent who needed no trick to become a winner.

Sondra took his outstretched hand, and granted him a hearty handshake. They followed him into a pleasant office, comfortable, but well furnished with electronics of the day, as well as books in a bookcase where a huge cut piece of dark green jade was used as a bookend.

Following her gaze Alt smiled. "Mr. Powell had aspirations to carve that hunk of jade. Said he could see a bear in there just waiting to get out…but he didn't have the time for it, I guess. It has always been there …He once told me it was Columbian Jade…I couldn't tell the difference. So, back to the electronics, I can, with a couple of fingers, pull up any information in seconds. Like anyone else the boss was frustrated when it didn't work, but he had hired a technician to keep all the devices in good working order and we were not often down."

Relieved, Sondra had access to the information she wanted; it was a well-run office and had been for many years. Caleb's desk had been kept polished, and her picture was there for all to see. With gratitude, she accepted a bottle of cool water and continued to interrogate both Rafe and Afton, until she was satisfied that she would change nothing in this office. Sondra never knew that Rafe slipped the jade into his briefcase with the intention of getting it carved.

At four o' clock the two of them left Afton carrying their tea tray out to the pantry. The routine would not change, the company would not fold and they would not all have to go job hunting. Afton could not have felt nobler, and it lasted for days. Job security was theirs.

"We now have a female Powell. But she is Caleb reincarnated," Afton said to his staff. "Nothing will change immediately."

In the heavy traffic Rafe considered stopping for a drink. He had managed the tea, but now weary, felt he could handle a cocktail. He said as much, but casually. He was not yet aware of Millicent's influence on Sondra. Did she frown on the social drink, he wondered.

"Would you like a cocktail, Sondra? There is a nice lounge coming up and I'd be happy to escort you. Quiet and crowded after the work day, but relaxing."

Sondra looked over at him. "I haven't done much socializing, but that sounds so good. Aunt Millie keeps sherry for us now…sometimes a bit before dinner or bedtime is in order. Yes. Let's do. If it's convenient. I've so many questions to ask now that I am beginning to see how it is all set up. It should transfer smoothly, so far as I can see. But I am sure—"

Rafe jerked, "What do you mean transfer? I don't understand."

"Well, if the San Francisco office is this well organized, I can see no reason to linger out here. I can transfer ownership rather simply, and get back to my life."

He swerved into a driveway, pulled around to a huge parking lot and handed his key to a valet. He came around to hold the door for her, and did his utmost to keep from exploding. He took her arm and led her into the cool, luxurious lounge filled with the after-work crowd. They were seated quickly but had to wait for a cocktail server

"Sondra, you have to realize that your life is over as you knew it up to the day Caleb died. Stop playing with the idea that you can hurt Caleb, he's dead.

It will be innocent people you destroy. You will lose big time—it will affect every move you make for years to come."

"Rafe. Whatever—" The cocktail server interrupted, took the order and returned with it, as the two of them sat speechless until Rafe took up his case once more.

"Hear me out. I have to warn you that you're trying to make a dangerous move." He moved his drink to the side. "Resentment has no place in this; intellectual capacity is required immediately. Powell Imports is a world-wide industry. Caleb Powell, shrewdly and with integrity, amassed a business worth millions of dollars, which he left to you, his biological daughter. A daughter who, whether you throw tantrums and insist you are not, *is his biological child*. Got that? Okay."

"Rafe, you are saying I am behaving like a spoiled brat."

"If the shoe fits, wear it. Yes. Sondra it is not about the money. It is not about you…you have no options without affecting the lives of millions of people… your own life will not be as restricted as you seem to believe. You have someone for every task there is. They are doing the finest job in the world. We've suffered no lawsuits; we've had nothing but the best of service from all of these employees…they do their job, why can't you do yours? Because you don't know what it is, do you? You've had to put your education to work on a small business scale…you are successful, now take it a step at a time with this big business. It will fall into place if you open your very good brain and admit the information, and process it with our guidance. You'll find that you *do not* have to run every office, every document and every life—and all that money—like your own personal bank account. It's not possible. Caleb knew it, he had Randall Everts. You will have Rand, too, if you chose—"

"All right! So being tied to a chair in a corporate office is a nightmare I don't want."

"You will be able to travel to foreign countries and meet your customer, and affiliates. At your own discretion. They'll invite you, expecting a business woman of integrity. I can't give it all to you at once, Sondy. You will have to make these discoveries. But you will make the decision to do it, or not to do it…follow Rand's guidance and you will love it, in time."

Sondra drained her glass and set it down, "On the advice of my corporation attorney, I submit. No more tantrums. Full speed ahead into the import business. Take me home, please."

"Yes, of course," was his grim reply.

Chapter Eleven

Rafe felt sick about what he'd done. But somehow she had to understand what she was facing and accept her birthright. What a bequest it was, too. "I felt almost like a father must feel when he has to tell his kid to stop throwing tantrums…she'll never forgive me. Ah well, at least I believe we will see the real Miss Powell very soon. And I will never be more than one of the queue of admirers." He shook his head, "Can't blame a guy for trying."

He drove back to the office, taking a detour to the Fenton Gallery where a young woman was Artist in Residence and left the jade with her. He had the promise of a bear. "I can see it!" she'd exclaimed, "It will take a few weeks, Rafe." And he left, muttering to himself, and went straight to his desk. He had some difficult litigation coming up…it was going to be a lot less stressful than buying Sondra Powell a cocktail and giving her fatherly advice on this dreary windy day.

The drive to get her home had been strained. They hadn't much more to say, and he had pleaded a full schedule of court cases awaiting him, and had driven away immediately. Thus, Sondra entered the quiet house alone; the kitchen had a few tools remaining to be cleared away, but there was no sight of Alma or Merilee.

A faint rustle from overhead, and she went upstairs to the bedrooms and found her aunt in one, involved in one of Sondra's ideas of renewal. Millicent was seated, carefully repairing several broken stitches of an old patch-quilt of velvet and brocade fabric in rich colors.

"We have to keep this one, Sondra. I can mend it safely. It has been cared for. You know, it was made by your Grandmother, Georgia Whitaker, as a wedding gift to Caleb and Susan. I thought we might use a duvet cover if it doesn't look right when I finish."

"This room has been finished. The new wallpaper is lighter, with those little bluebells and yellow daisies…don't they make those covers in prints? That wouldn't work…"

"Have to see. I am glad you don't want to store it somewhere."

"If it can be salvaged, cleaned and used, we will keep everything we possibly can. I want to finish checking out the house. I need to see if the dining room is finished."

The airiness and cheerfulness of the bedrooms was a comfort to her. At least it was no longer what she had considered nightmare alley on these upper floors. Just a little paint, fabric and letting in the light was all it needed. She headed down the stairs to the kitchen once more.

She was pleased to see that the bow window was in the frame. In a couple of days they would finish the outside to look like it had always been there, which it could have been from some photographs she had seen. She grabbed an apple from the bowl of fruit on the counter, and went to the library. "High expectations," she murmured.

She smiled widely; the tall window was installed. Men on the outside were finishing their tasks. Well and good; the permit had arrived and the exterior was due to be painted in two days. She felt a bit of excitement at the thought of how much better it would appear to passersby.

Ok. So, a trip to the dining room…nothing had been done. She was exasperated. "Gary Toppel," she called out.

She heard him coming down the stairs.

"You're home," he said.

"What's the status on the wallpaper in the dining room?"

"Got to hire a hanger for that. I don't do paper. I'll try to get them here by the weekend."

"Tell you what," Sondra said decisively. "Have you someone to help me with the job? I can get it done in about four hours. Everything is there waiting—"

His mouth flew open, "You? Hang wallpaper? I don't think so."

She stared him down. "I have done entire houses, for your information. With the aid of a nice young man who provided the extra hands…so get it prepped for me, can you? I'll go get changed and be right down." *Ah. Thank goodness, we did not get into a fight.*

Papa's Jade

In fifteen minutes Sondra clattered down the stairs in an old snug fitting pair of jeans with an old plaid shirt only a man would have owned, and pink sneakers. Her hair was caught up in plastic clips to keep it out of the way; she was turning to work with a vengeance. She'd show that dunderhead Gary Toppel.

In the dining room, the ladder was up, the bucket of water was waiting, and the rolls of pre-pasted paper were stacked on the large sheets of paper that lined the floor. Cloths, large brushes and a plastic smoother, cutting knife and level and yardstick…she inventoried quickly and was satisfied. She might have inherited millions, but she could still work. And she meant to do just that.

She was measuring the first strip when she became aware that Toppel was standing in the doorway watching. "That your boyfriend's shirt?"

He stepped over to help with the measuring, brushing against her, touching her hands.

"No. It was my uncle Wallace's. Millie found two shirts still in the package, in a drawer after all his stuff was cleared out—when he died. I liked this one and she gave it to me."

He grunted, "A helper is on the way. He had to go wash up. I had to pull him off the job…getting the siding back in place. I like the colors you chose for the exterior. Like you say, it will keep the style but look much better. And it will be edible—butterscotch is good candy."

She suppressed a laugh, "Thanks. I once did one in New York for a family who chose an almost identical color to the burgundy on this one. I never did like it but they were crazy about it. You won't believe it, but they wanted pink on the millwork…so they let me redo it in white and I added a few drops of the burgundy to change the white subtly. Turned out perfect."

"Here's Louis. He will do what you tell him to do." He spoke for her only and was gone.

"Great," Sondra said without looking up. She made her first cut, went to the tray of water to prepare the strip. "I need you to help keep this from folding and buckling."

"Yes, ma'am, I can do that."

She looked up into the gentle face, startled.

"Don't be afraid of it, I'll get the idea on this first one," he assured quietly.

He was at least forty, but something was missing. Her heart twisted as she recognized a veteran of some recent battle who might or might not ever be whole again.

"I learn fast, Miss Powell. I saw this done once, so I believe we can work together."

"Fine, Louis. Here we go, I make these folds like this…"

"Yeah, I can do the ladder thing, if you like. Get it nice and straight at the top. Got the brush ready."

"I am anxious to see if this horrible green is going to show through, let me get this first one…then you will get a turn."

The strip went up and her helper waited until she began smoothing then got a brush and went behind her making sure to prevent bubbles and wrinkles. It was going up fast. It was adhering. It was beautiful.

"Thank you, God," she whispered. The paper was dense and there was no evidence of the horrid green beneath it. "I'll call that green goo the primer coat of paint. That'll make Gary happy."

By Saturday Sondra had recovered from the dining room task. It was as perfect and satisfying as she had expected. Still Victorian setting, but with an uplifting lightness, although nothing changed. The china was the same, the lace at the windows was fresh and clean, the pictures were going back up and artifacts were being replaced as she satisfied her love of light and order.

Painters had begun preparing the exterior of the house, and would be transforming the place during the next week. Considering that the roof shingles were dark rust colored, she had chosen a paint color called Butterscotch, the millwork would be done in Light Ivory, and for the fine line-of-emphasis trim around the windows and doors she had chosen a dark reddish-brown.

She was proud that the new windows were already fitting in as if they had always been there. But her major accomplishment was the bow window and breakfast area in the kitchen. It had always been there, it just needed Sondy Powell to uncover it, said Millicent.

They found the perfect breakfast set—a forty inch round oak table with four matching chairs—by slipping out to antique shops. No one had any idea where they were, and they laughed at Merilee's scolding when they returned. Delivered the next day, the set was perfect for the subtle green kitchen with bisque appliances, which seemed to smile when they added a pale white and yellow print gauze curtain, held back with orange and green twisted cord. A white stoneware pitcher of yellow daisies and multicolor tulips stood proudly in the center of a crocheted doily, on the oak table.

"Rand sent them this morning," Merilee said, "his card said for the kitchen table."

"Well that man is full of surprises," Millicent laughed.

All was well. Day by day Sondra was being briefed on the workings of the company and her part as owner. It was a daunting task awaiting her, but she could still recall the *'spoiled child'* evaluation of Rafe's that day over drinks, and only the martini had gotten her through without making a mess of things. Being unused to alcoholic drinks, that one had fortified her, it had spared her everything but hurt… Now the spoiled child was taking a new look at herself.

She spent time with Afton, and often with Rafe as he filled her in on the legalities. So much to take in, but she reminded herself that there were people in positions to take care of any needs, all they had to do was report to the main office…so that left San Francisco.

Rand had called once or twice, he was preparing for her arrival and takeover as carefully as he could. He would come for her Thursday. They would travel back together in his personal vehicle, a Nissan sedan, if that was acceptable to her.

True to his word, Rand arrived Thursday, hoping that she had finally come to terms with her state of affairs, and that it would not be temporary. Once she had finished with the house transformation, would she again declare that she would go home? Well, good enough, he thought. I've got another house for her…maybe, just maybe…

He got the surprise of his life when he found her in his own suite of rooms, in which she had created a haven for him that was the quintessence of peace—something he found little of in his career which constantly demanded decisions of unlimited importance. Sondra had her back to him, as she was adjusting new drapes. How, he wondered had she stayed well below budget with what she had obviously accomplished? This looked as expensive as the devil.

"Hello Rand." He jerked in surprise, "Glad you are here safely…I need one more week to finish this job, please. Then I will be moving to San Francisco—I plan to spend one week, full time, at the office. After that, I will begin on the house there; however, I will give you four hours a day…probably early morning, until I have either redecorated or sold Powell House."

"Sell? Powell House in 'Frisco..." he gasped, and wanting a moment to recover, he replaced his black leather chair in the exact same place, the couch had not been moved. Everything remained masculine, although she had reversed the colors; the walls from beige to a subtle terra cotta; the trim to light beige in a few places, but she had not changed any of the few black articles in the place. In fact, *she had* done away with his footstool and a little side table and replaced it with black lacquered—but these were the same ones! They were his personal ones from leaner days when pine or some other less expensive wood was one's choice! And what the heck had she done at the window?

He blew out his breath, "I really do like this, Sondy. It is the same, but—wow! I do like it all...the drapes." He waved his arm.

Two panels of beige drapery were designed with squares of plaid strewn randomly, never touching and angled differently. Scattered, like the wind is blowing them, he thought. His mouth opened, how did she find the fabric in the exact colors she'd used throughout? He looked up to see a swag edged in forest green braid and watched as she tied the panels back with the same green tasseled braid that had always been there—as had the ivory lace underneath. He frowned, it was the same but it was not, it was light...He stared at her, as something quickened in him.

"You seem speechless. But then, you have never seen my work, have you?"

"Tell me, why would you want to do something as grand as you've done with this house, and then sell it?"

"This will remain with us. We have people here who need the work, and we can afford to keep them here. Perhaps someday I'll raise my children here... I suspect Aunt Millicent will prefer to stay here...her happiest memories are in this house." She paused, replaced some reading material on the table and turned, "What would you say to the idea of something benevolent being done here? I am thinking of scholarships for special students, awarding them board and room and a small income while enrolled and working toward a worthwhile career? It is something I think we should consider."

"You are suddenly the executive...are you staying? What the devil has happened? I was almost resigned to your rejection, and now this. I, I don't know about that idea. Let me get my breath. Caleb had his own ideas... occasionally."

"It seems that the brat has seen the errors of her thinking. So, I am about to become head of a corporation. You," she pointed at him, "will be there with me all the way, 'till death do us part'…If you ever think of leaving me in a lurch, I will, I will—I don't know what, but I will."

"Did we just get married? That sounded like a permanent commitment, or was it just a threat."

"Uh, no, I meant to say that you are to remain CEO permanently, until I decide to make you my partner…in the company."

Rand raised shaking hands to his head, wiped through his hair and exhaled loudly. "Okay, Miss Powell. You are in. You can have your week, then you are mine. All mine in 'Frisco. I will introduce you to the world Caleb Powell created and watch you put your own spin on that. It is going to be quite a life. Welcome to the corporate world…So, I've already seen to your own personal income…it's in the bank, your checks are on the way. Our accountant will keep your statement for you, and if you get close to overspending he will notify you so he can take care of depositing funds for you."

"What? I have an account in Newark…oh. I understand. And that's another thing, Rand. I wonder how it would be to incorporate SG Interior Designs in Powel Imports. I could find a competent CEO to handle it back there, couldn't I?"

"Sondy, get together with Rafe and see which way will be best to go with the small business. Meantime, get together with your manager and keep in touch, maybe even fly back to visit, if you wish." *She didn't even ask what her salary was going to be.*

"Will I ever be free to go home again? I would like to go back and thank them all for such loyalty. They were responsible for our success and deserve more than a sell-out…"

"You will be able to go wherever you wish, Sondra. You own Powell Imports, do not let the company own you."

"Yes, well—"

"Sondy—oh, hello Rand. Nice to see you again." Millicent stood with a huge bundle in her hands. "Darling this just came special delivery. I gave the courier a fiver from the cash in the drawer. He seemed happy, anyway. It's the blue velvet draperies. This is only one package, of course, they were too heavy…and you've got to see this. They restored the color…" She opened a slit to reveal the gorgeous cotton velvet in all of its Wedgewood blue glory."

They almost forgot Rand as they placed the package on his bed and opened it. The clock had been turned back, yet the fabric was restored, and someone had given it fresh new lining; then, as he watched and wondered at the folds, Millicent laughed and said, "Don't look so puzzled, Rand. She found a place that not only restored the color, but pleated these over-drapes that will open and close with a pull cord. And with them open you get to see the beautiful side yard."

Rand sighed, now he understood. Sondra had not gone all out spending money on a project but had saved not only material in this old house, she had preserved many memories, as well. Rand Everts could not stop himself from falling in love with this wondrous woman, who had a temper, determination and, for all her pain over the years, she was not selfish and introverted.

"Hey, everyone," Merilee called from the doorway, "we've brought fast food…only one time guys…the kitchen is about clean enough to go back to meal preparation. Lunch in the dining room today, outa cartons and wrappers. Come down in about ten minutes."

"Oops, almost forgot. Judge Powell called. She wants you to call her. "

Rand blinked. The doorway was empty. "Fast food? I don't know…."

Millicent said, "I think we will be safe, if we make them start first."

"Millie—" Sondra laughed, "Be nice. How many times did we have a burger and fries when we were struggling? Aha, do not forget, love."

Rand looked at them both, and realized how difficult life had been for them. Sondra Powell was a strong woman; she wasn't pampered. Sue Lee Powell was who she should be. Caleb Powell knew exactly what he was doing.

Chapter Twelve

The next day, when Sondra called her, Sue Lee answered in a panic, "Oh, Sis, I can't make it on Saturday. I think I can make it by noon on Sunday. We should be home by then…Will that work for you?"

Sondy laughed, "Yes, We're home from church by noon…I—I like it when you call me that—Sis, and sister."

"It is fun, isn't it? I have always needed to have someone of my own, and you were always there, a sweet smelling baby who laughed and played with me…but, now, it is okay for me to come Sunday? I do need to try on that dress I saw, if we agree I can use it. If it needs altering or is not usable, I'll need time to get one made."

"That takes weeks, doesn't it? Let's hope this one you want fits."

"James insists we are to be married in a little Baptist church he found. You know, we go there almost every Sunday. I really do like the sermons. They are thought provoking. It's sort of like going to Sunday School."

"Aunt Millie and I went to a small church near our house…the people there were so loving, I really do miss them. But, whatever, yes, come when you can on Sunday. I'll wait for you."

"Bye, then. Give your Aunt my love."

Sondra sat for a few moments, letting the new feeling wash over her. Sister. How wrong she had been to dislike Sue Lee. She got up, and wandered into the parlor (never called living room in this style house) and studied it once more. The Cherrywood had been used in here but it was a desk, which puzzled her as to its usefulness when there was a library in the house. She later learned that her mother kept it there so she could write little notes and be readily available to callers during certain hours. The wall covering was a strange color silk—pink, maybe? Not so…just something dark with dirty looking flowers in the design. "Oh, my," she sighed, "age was not kind to you."

She hurried to get her note pad. The settee with two Victorian Rococo side chairs would remain. The brocade upholstery was in good shape and the colors would be good to work with. Everything else could be kept, but she would have to decide upon new drapes in here. In her mind the delicate lavender-grey background from the print upholstery was the color for the walls. Perhaps a shade darker would do for the window dressing. Again, tiebacks, and gentle swags edged with a bit of braid in elderberry wine color over white lace panels filled her mind and she nodded. The wine and grey carpet would remain. They had faded to the colors she could use easily.

For now, she set aside her notes and picked up an apple in the kitchen, then headed for the attic. She had wedding dresses to locate.

Sondra climbed the stairs to the attic in search of some history. The dresses and everything else had to be up here. Everything they ever owned would be there somewhere. Attics were notorious for yielding the dark secrets, and happiness of a house. She knew that from experience.

There was no light switch at the landing. She could see a chain hanging from an overhead light bulb, pulled it and was startled at the amount of light it gave off. She could see the stairs clearly, and the landing, small as it was, had ample visibility. "I've seen them all, now," she murmured, recalling the homes she had redone in past years.

The usual memorabilia was abandoned to this dark dusty place. She looked right at a steamer trunk that was covered with stickers: PEKING CHINA; OCEAN TRAVEL TO THE ORIENT; THE GREAT WALL; U.S.OF A., SHIPPING AND TOURIST LINES. And there was one significant pennant in white and gold that said only, Honeymoon 1954.

Everywhere she looked were trunks, and boxes taped to keep out the dust and seal up the treasures within. A dressmaker's dummy with a tiny waist was covered with a sheet. In a corner stood a large covered something that she thought might be a bed, but turned out to be art work in a rack, paintings signed by H. Powell. Uncertain about who the artist was, she could not visualize using any of them in this house; however, she did consider them desirable landscapes that perhaps should be sold, or given to museums.

Turning to a final inspection, she saw that there was one old sewing machine, some small furnishings, stacks of sealed cartons, fishing gear, a rusted bicycle, and an interesting box with a baseball bat, tennis racket, and balls. *No bowling pins?*

A huge carton bridged between two chairs was nearly six feet long, at least four feet wide. It was deep enough to hold a body...Sondra gasped, and read the writing on the label. Elijah and Hilda Johnson Powell Wedding August 10, 1890. Hilda had lived to meet Sondra but died at eighty-eight soon after Millicent left, taking Sondra with her.

She ripped off the tape. Her grandmother's wedding dress was intact. It was a heavy white taffeta.

Sondra lifted it out and held it across her arms. There was no scent of moth balls or perfume, it was in excellent condition. Taking it up by the shoulders she checked it out: sweetheart neckline bodice overlaid in lace; dropped waist, and turning she stared at the bustle of ruffles which also cascaded down the edge of the train. She laid it across the box, took off her jeans, slipped out of her knit top and began undoing the buttons on the dress. She stood tall to settle the dress over her head and ease her arms into the long, slim lace sleeves. She pressed the dress into place, and holding the front against her chest she took a few steps. Her heart fluttered when she realized it was a perfect fit for her. Her grandmother must have been her size. Looking around she did not see a mirror so she picked up the skirt and went down to the first bedroom on the lower floor.

A stranger faced her when she stepped up to the full length mirror. She tilted her head; she turned but the back was not fastened, yet she got a good look at the bustle effect. She reached back to adjust the train. Not too long, she thought. Again she looked into the mirror. *This is the dress Sue Lee wants.*

Her bubble burst. "Mummy," she whispered. "This wasn't yours. Where is yours? It was—did Aunt Millie say it was cotton *tiers*...oh, no. I have to find it."

Sondra quickly returned to the attic, removed the precious gown and replaced it, complete with wrappings, and some of the tape held once more. Looking around she realized that there were so many places her mother's dress could be.

She pulled on her jeans and top, reset her hair with the cloisonné trimmed clips, and went to the trunk with the labels on them. The lock snapped open after a couple of forceful tries, and she caught her breath at the contents.

Dresses, lingerie, shoes, handbags and gloves. And a silk dressing gown of delicate sheerness, fine lawn fabric in summer dresses of ruffles and ribbons and embroidery of the finest needles. Of course, this was her mother's trousseau. But where was the wedding dress Aunt Millie had described?

She replaced the tissue, and closed and locked the chest.

Looking around she noticed another chest atop a table. She hesitated, but then feeling drawn to open it she found what she had been looking for—her mother's belongings, pictures, books and other accessories beneath the prudently wrapped gown. She lifted it out and laid it atop the large trunk. She loosened the tape and opened the protective paper. Atop the dress was a large white envelope. Her hands shook as she opened the envelope and found studio portraits, dated nineteen-fifty-four, of Caleb and Susan Powell's wedding.

A small picture fell to the floor; she picked it up gently. It was a family picture…three years later. She moaned, and sat on the floor with a thump. No one had to tell her that it was her family. Caleb was standing, and Susan was seated, holding Sondra who in turn was staring out in wonder at the photographer. It was dated on her second birthday.

Sondra sat crying for a long time. However even sorrow had its limits. Presently, she stood up and after wiping her eyes and blowing her nose, she began replacing everything. That's where it all belongs, she decided. There's no need to punish yourself with the sight of what might have been by keeping it under foot. *You can't go back and bring it to life.*

When she had replaced everything and closed the chest, she admitted to herself that they were telling her the truth about Caleb. She watched a black spider scuttle across the floor and up the wall, and she was suddenly determined to fulfill Caleb's dream for her. She would not fail him.

"I'll go look for journals, Caleb's or even Susan's. The library, surely they would be there," she whispered as the spider disappeared. For now, she had to finish the house and go to her destiny in San Francisco. *Oh, heavens. I forgot Rand was here! He'll think I neglect him.*

Sondra would have been horrified to know that Everts had come up the steps earlier, and stayed quietly watching her for about fifteen minutes before he turned and went down the stairs.

She closed the door, pulled the chain on the light and headed back down.

Where was everyone? The house was empty of workers, Alma and Merilee were not in their quarters and Aunt Millicent was nowhere to be found. At last, a small note on the refrigerator caught her eye, "Couldn't find you. Gone out to dinner—Rand is taking me. Alma and Merilee are over at their old apartment cleaning one last time. Your dinner is in the refrigerator. Home soon. Love Millie."

Before she could check out the cold meal, the doorbell rang and she hurried to open the door which had not been painted, and she was startled to see that it was almost dark outside. She had a decision to make about that heavy old ornate door—she opened it and Sue Lee grinned at her mischievously. She held out two takeout dinners in cartons.

"Hi, is it too late for us to see the gown? I couldn't wait until tomorrow. I brought roast beef dinners with extra gravy. We can heat everything in the microwave, I'm good at that."

They hugged, despite the food between them. They laughed and the evening was theirs to make the most of. They had much to share with each other, and did so enthusiastically over their meal. Finally, eager to get to the wedding dress, they left their debris on the table in the kitchen nook and hurried up the stairs to the attic. Sue Lee reached up to pull the light chain. "I was so glad when Gem had our handyman put a longer chain on this light. I couldn't reach it before. Yeah, you guessed it, I spent a lot of time up here. I'll have to show you the doll house, I think it was meant for you, but no one seemed to mind if I played with it…"

With plenty of light just where they needed it, they went in, Sue Lee went directly to the box, opened it and in seconds had the dress in her hands. Holding it up, she said, "Isn't it the most delicious dress? A little yellowed on the bustle and ruffles, but it enhances it I think. I don't know whose it was…not your mom's I think…do you know?"

"Put it on, Sue. Yes, I was just coming down from looking at it when you arrived. It is a gorgeous one, pretty old but I think it will hold up well—here, let me do up the buttons in the back…I found some information and photo's in another place. This was Grandmother Hilda Powell's dress. She and Elijah were married in August 1890."

"Oh, no!" gasped Sue Lee. "I can't wear this, it is an heirloom for you. Not me."

"It is an heirloom for you. You were adopted. We are sisters, despite the way Caleb kept us apart. You do have a right…and a responsibility to your own English mother to enjoy the use of this dress. Now, we won't even have to do a thing to alter it. You won't want to have it cleaned, Sue Lee. It might not take today's handling...Just hang it to air for a while...oh you are dazzling in this. You look like a queen. Wow! James will eat you up."

"That dangerous, huh? Maybe I better go buy a polyester dress."

They both heard Millicent call, "Sondra where are you? Is that black car on the drive Sue Lee's? Rand said it might be. Is she here? Come out, wherever you two are."

Sondra went to the door, called down and turned back to help Sue Lee out of the dress. They carefully settled it back in the box, and "Okay if I take it tonight? I won't let James see it...bad luck, I think. He thinks I might want to go Chinese and wear a red dress...in a Christian Church...no way, I am not that dumb."

"Well," Sondra drawled, "Then you might honor that heritage with a red garter for your stocking. Not red underthings...they might show through...everything white, Sunny."

Sue Lee giggled, "Can't have that, tempting as it is. Maybe a red nighty...."

They went downstairs to Rand, Millicent and the two tired homemakers, and the evening closed early. Rand carried the precious gown out for Sue Lee, in its carton, slipped it into the back seat of the black car and watched Sue Lee drive away smiling. He asked, "What the heck was in that box?"

"Oh, her wedding dress. She will be wearing our Grandmother Hilda's from eighteen ninety. Wait until you see it. Stunning."

"*Our* grandmother?"

"Yes. Grandmother Hilda Johnson Powell."

Rand stared at her in the glare of the porch light, he moved closer, reached up and traced her cheek with his finger, softly. "What has happened to you? Can I hope you are waking up finally, Sleeping Beauty?"

"Could be." Sondra murmured as she reached up defensively; their hands collided and Rand took hers and held it to his mouth. He kissed her fingers.

"Welcome to the real world, Sondra Powell...I've got to go. I *will* come for you the week after next..." In the next breath, he asked, "What are you going to do with that ugly front door?"

She frowned. "It does have to go...on the other hand, I want to see if it can be redesigned with a window in it. I think the Carmine—reddish brown—might be a good color to use. There's not much trim...a frosted window with floral bouquet would do well. Yes, thanks. That's my last task. I pronounce the house finished."

With a little tug, Rand pulled her closer, bent his head and settled his lips on hers. Gently, softly, he held it. He lifted his head. "I'll see that door later. Take care, Sondy Powell. I'm leaving now, driving back to 'Frisco. Good night."

He left her standing with her hand on her lips. "Good night, Rand." She whispered. She heard the car door close, the engine started and the tail lights flashed as he drove away. She felt the coolness of nights in Sacramento, and was not sure she had ever felt such emotion before.

"What was that all about, Sondy?"

"Oh. Aunt Millie. I—Rand just took off for San Francisco…we were talking about the front door."

"Is that right? I was seeing things, then. I thought he kissed you."

Sondra sighed. "Yes, he did. It was…it was just a friendly gesture. He is happy that I finally have decided to stay."

"And are you, my darling? You gave Hilda's wedding dress to Sue Lee…that was generous of you. You didn't have to do that, you know."

"Yes, yes I did, Millie. It's her heritage, too. She's my sister, you know. Adopted, but legally my sister."

"Well, wherever he is, Caleb must be very satisfied that he did the right thing with the two of you. I imagine he is self-righteously saying 'that is the way it should have been'."

"Let's go in, Millie. I need to clean up our dinner things in the kitchen. And I want to look for some books in the library…it's about bedtime, too."

"So," Sondra said as she took her aunt by the arm, "what have you been up to today? And dinner out with Rand…you are being social out here, aren't you."

"Wait until I tell you about something I was thinking…oh, what will you do with the front door? I am tired of that ugly thing."

Sondra explained in detail; they went inside and closed the ugly door which did not know it was destined for splendor, that it would have an elegant frosted glass window with lilies, and a swan, and ribbons and vines and leaves. And that Millicent would love it.

Chapter Thirteen

At ten o'clock on Wednesday morning, the doorbell rang. Merilee answered it to the media; cars and cameras were on the drive, the street, and even up on the lawn. Her welcoming smile vanished as she learned why they were here… to get Miss Sondra Powell's statement about a riot.

"I've no idea what you are talking about," she frowned, and started to close the door.

He was persistent. He stretched out his arm to prevent it. "Come on, lady. She owns the company. She has to have something to say about last night on the docks at San Francisco."

"You need to go to the company in San Francisco, then. You've got no business digging in here, this is a house of mourning…there'll be no statements from here."

"That's not the information we have. Mourning? More like she's renovating this place. Word is that Miss Powell owns SG Interior Decorating Company in New Jersey. Now that she has inherited Powell Imports, she's living at this mansion. We need a statement from her. About the protest against Powell Imports' dealings with China."

"Get yourself out of the doorway, and I will see if Miss Powell will see you. But not that crowd out there. Tell them to leave, only one reporter and camera to remain."

"I don't have control of them…"

"Then remove your arm from the door before I call the police to come take away a bunch of people trying to harass the recently bereaved owner of this house."

He dropped his arm, and shook his head. "If that's the way you want it, but you are going to regret this."

"That will be my problem, now won't it?"

Merilee closed the door and locked it. She could see through the frosted window as he turned and wended his way through the crowd which, in a few moments, followed suit. In moments the disgruntled crowd was gone.

"Merilee, honey," Alma whispered from beside her, "You better go tell Sondra about this immediately. You've got to…she doesn't need any surprises when she goes out and about."

"What surprises don't I need, ladies?" Sondra was on her way out. "I love surprises, most of them anyway."

"You won't like this one," Alma murmured.

Startled, Sondra asked, "What is it? What's going on?"

Merilee blurted out the entire event. Sondra listened, her eyes opened wide, "Why in the world didn't you call me immediately?—never mind. I can take care of this." She whirled around and went to the library. She called Rafe's office, but his receptionist informed her that he had an emergency at Powell Imports and had flown to San Francisco an hour earlier. She could try him there.

The circuits were busy, of course. She had to get through. She had a private number for what was now her office, and Rand answered immediately. "Sondra, can you call me later? We have a little situation here—"

"That's why I'm calling. Reporters were just here and Merilee handled it badly. Not sure that I would have handled it either, since I have no information about a riot on the docks. What has that to do with us? The reporter said they were protesting Powell Import's agreement with China or something."

"Ok. Here's the brief. A group of twenty or so young couples from a local church group were protesting our dealings with China. Our Security Officer, Henry Jakes, had a time convincing them that they need to take their protest to their federal representatives who can make the decisions about that. It seems they were concerned about so much being imported when we need jobs here at home. They did not know that attacking one company was useless…we got them convinced and they started leaving, but someone had called the police and it was a tussle getting them out. Some of the spokesmen were arrested… Sondra I need to go. We have it under control. You might want to call a news conference immediately and set them straight, with apologies for being turned away. You'll know what to say. Just not too much. Okay? I *will* call you later, when I can have time to talk about this."

That was it. She replaced the phone and sat down for a few minutes. Resolutely, she looked up a major newspaper and dialed. When she had gone through a couple of people, she was connected to the Editor in Chief. "You have some complaint, lady, take it to the complaint department."

"This is Sondra G. Powell—"

He interrupted, "New head of Powell Imports? The subscription department can get you on the list for delivery—"

"Your people were at my front door this morning." She interrupted, overlooking his rudeness for the moment, "As well as almost fifty reporters creating chaos. My housekeeper turned them away. We were, after all in mourning, not aware of the events…I thought it expedient to contact you, but if you are not receptive to my call, I can contact another media."

When she further indicated that she was granting him an exclusive interview, he turned on his charm. She gave him only the information she wanted printed, and warned him against speculating in the articles.

"You sound like a sensible man, a fair man, and I am confiding that I was not involved until a few minutes ago. You have my permission to print the following statement: I have not assumed my responsibility with Powell Imports; however, I have been in contact with our Chief Executive Officer, Randall Everts and am aware of the event. It is being handled by company officials in San Francisco. Any further contact must be with that office."

"When will you be taking over in San Francisco?"

"That is undecided at this moment. Perhaps within two weeks."

"Thanks, Miss Powell."

"Mr. Basillo, harassment by the press is really not appreciated. I value highly our freedom of press, TV and movies, but not fabrications, or intimidating articles about me or my life. I am a working woman and, just as the workers in the media would not like to have derogatory statements about them appear in the media, I value my privacy also."

"Thanks, Miss Powell. Sorry for the attitude…we have a Special Edition going out at three 'o'clock. I truly appreciate your call giving us this exclusive. I will use only your quote in a brief article."

Sondra replaced the phone and sat quietly. What had she gotten into? "I'll never be able to handle this responsibility." She murmured.

"But of course you will. You just did a splendid job, darling." Aunt Millicent was sitting nearby in a huge chair that almost swallowed her. She got up, "Let me get you a sip of sherry. You are pale as a ghost. It's your first real test of life on top of the mountain." She was back in seconds with the glass and it was just a mouthful. Sondra sipped at until it was gone.

"Now what is this all about, Sondy? You called Rand? Well, you both did very well." She turned to leave, "I really need to get some things done. I thought I would tackle that attic now, and get rid of some of the weight on that floor. I saw stuff that should have been sent out to charities long ago…trust me, I will keep the things of value to the family history. I'll set up some semblance of order—and I am extremely good at finding articles to send out to auction, you will recall."

"You darling," Sondra hugged her aunt. "I was going to go shopping and get a couple of things for the office…California clothes. But I don't think I *will* go out just now."

"Might not be safe. You don't want to deal again with the media. You never know how it will turn out…" She was out the door, and Sondra could hear her steps on the stairs.

Rafe called just before dinner. He was in San Francisco, and she was again in the library searching for some sort of inventory of the books and artifacts. There was no organization at all, reference books beside classic novels…somewhere there was a librarian for hire, she thought.

"It's over." Rafe said. "We didn't have time to bring you in on this. I had a 'copter bring me down, when Rand called." He repeated what Rand had told her, but added his own tidbit. "So, it went sour for them, but they did not intend the riot. You always have trouble makers in those kinds of crowds. Couple of professional riot-makers set it off, someone called the police and they scuffled a bit. Media was right in the middle of it and it looked pretty bad for about forty-five minutes."

"And how is everything now? Will there be further trouble?"

"I don't think so. This is the action of an uninformed group. Don't see it happening again. So, I am on my way home. I'll see you soon."

Sondra Powell was not politically inclined. She did her duty and voted, researched her candidates and, on occasion, had redecorated the home of a Senator and a Governor. But no favors had been suggested…they were not flaunting their careers to her and asking for support. She was disturbed by the event, but the media was fair and when it was over, she looked for the news stories to find out how it had been resolved. She found nothing, and in time wrote in her journal, closed it and forgot the event.

Something non-related took her attention several days later. Two men, obviously Asian, who spoke broken English appeared at their door, and Merilee had taken them to the parlor and asked them to be seated. She went for Sondra who was in the kitchen with Alma, making brownies.

"Oh, my I wasn't expecting anyone… I'm glad I took time to dress in something other than jeans. This dress is not new, but a blue shirtwaist is always presentable… I wonder what they could want." She hurried to the parlor.

"I am Sondra Powell, gentlemen. Please be seated." She indicated the settee. "What brings you to my home? Perhaps you wish to see Sue Lee Powell, or Mrs. Chang?"

With the usual politeness they were apologetic for disturbing her. And no, they did not know either of those persons. They were in her home because it was said that an article of rare jade had been given to Caleb Powel in nineteen fifty-four and, "we would request the permission to view such an object. We are in charge of reclaiming artifacts for the museums of our homeland, China."

"That is a remarkable venture, gentlemen. But although I have heard the same story, I have never been aware of such an existence." She shrugged. "It is easy for people to make up stories about such as this. I am certain my father, Caleb Powell, would have kept it safe and cared for something so sacred…if he did indeed ever receive such an object. However, I am certain he would never purchase values of another country. It was not in his interest."

"It is our information that he was given a valuable statue in reward for taking away a child of mixed race. The jade, from the Ch'ing Dynasty must be returned to its rightful place."

Sondra stood up, and they both got to their feet, "I am sorry. I have no idea how such a story got started. My mother would never have allowed such a thing. She was with him. They had done the proper thing, adopting the little child whose mother was English and had died. I really cannot do more for you. I am sorry. Someone, I think, has given you some information that has no truth, perhaps."

They bowed slightly. "Thank you, Miss Powell. We would hope that if you discover you have been kept uninformed of this matter and come upon such an object, you would be kind enough to notify this person at once." The shorter of the two handed her a card with a name and phone number; it was official looking. "We have great desire to see our treasures restored to us."

"But of course. I understand. I will do as you ask, if it should happen—this way, Gentlemen." In the foyer, Sondra put the card in the lacquered dish on the mahogany table. The Geisha figurine of jadeite remained in its place.

She closed the door behind them and went inside. "I didn't really lie. I have never seen that jade they talk about. I can't say for sure that it still exists. I have no idea where it could be. It hasn't turned up in any of the safes or the bank, here. I wouldn't even know what it looks like…"

"What looks like?" Alma asked as Sondra rejoined her.

"Some jade statue. They think it's a true story about Sue Lee's father giving Caleb Powell a jade artifact. Oh, forget it. I plan to."

"Never heard such a thing. Been in this house most of ten years now, with Gem and Sue Lee. Nothing ever said, never saw anything like that. Jade, you say. No. Nothing to that story. I wonder what they were really looking for. Can't ever tell when strangers come asking questions you can't answer—now here's how I bake my brownies"—she went into a length lecture on how to do it so that it comes out more cake-like. "Not so many calories. You could even eat two."

Sondra laughed, poured the batter into the nine-inch pan and placed it in the oven to bake. She set the timer, and went to clean up while Alma started to work on the next meal.

It was a dusty, disheveled Millicent who came to Sondra in the library an hour later. She was struggling with a huge plastic lawn bag and perspiration had streaked down her forehead. She raised a hand to wipe it away and groaned. "I'll never be clean again."

"Millie. What on earth?"

"Take a look in here. See if you agree that this can go to The Thrift Shop—their proceeds go to veteran's hospitals. They will come and pick it up in the morning. Seemed glad to get it. Joseph, their man, said if we had old hats and furs and stuff they would give them to a Little Theater Group that can use period costumes."

"Was any of this marked?" Sondra opened the bag and was amazed at the collection of old castoffs. "I'm thinking we must keep some things to offer to a local historical museum. They might be interested in Elijah and Hilda Powell's things…"

Papa's Jade

"Oh, this was just in unmarked boxes, some were in a waste basket, and there was a laundry basket with shoes and purses from a very long time ago. I dusted and washed stuff...Look at these ankle boots—Oh, No!"

"What? Is something wrong, Millie?"

"I wonder if these were the ones Susan wore for her wedding...but these are not white...no, okay. I nearly had a stroke. Hers are probably in with the dress and stuff. That's logical, isn't it?"

"We'll set them aside, just to be sure," Sondra offered. She dropped them down beside a chair. "This looks good to go. Be sure you went through these purses...might be love letters or even money in them."

"I will look for love letters. The money they can have. Somebody needs it now more than we do." Millie grunted, picked up the tied bag and headed for the foyer.

Sondra shook her head, she stretched and twisted her head, and as she did so she looked up to the uppermost shelf of books. She stopped, frowning, then finished her exercise and stood staring up at the shelf. She counted six random volumes of some encyclopedia set—incomplete, and unusual, she thought. As uncommon as the object being used as a book end. Maybe a sea shell or rock of sentimental value to Caleb. There was a step stool at hand, she got up on it and reached for the first volume which was B to C She replaced that one, pushed aside the heavy bookend and, then took the second one. It was F to G. "Senseless," she murmured. Or was it? She examined the volume, it opened with a bit of effort and she stared at the discovery of a delicate gold and diamond necklace embedded in white velvet. The volume was a jewelry box! She reached for the second one and came up with a duplicate only smaller, like one designed for a child....when she had recovered she saw the engraved tab of gold, Susan...and Sondra.

She replaced everything, got down and looked for a chair. Groping, processing, and feeling the grief swell in her chest.

She settled in the desk chair and, stunned by her discovery, automatically reached out for the ringing phone.

"Sondra," said a familiar voice, "sorry I was unable to visit with you when you called. It was some situation we had here."

She was unable to answer at once, but managed to take a breath. "Is everything all right now? I hope that is the end of riots...Rand, I have so much to tell you...yes, I'll be ready. It's time I put in an appearance at Powell Imports.

And you won't believe what happened this morning. What I just found on the top shelf of the bookcase...."

"Snoopy little thing. What do you think of the necklaces?"

"You know about it? Are they safe there? I put them back...replaced that ugly rock."

"Yes, they are...I know everything. I told you, he worshiped the two of you."

She swallowed, and sighed, "Something else happened. You don't know about this. Two Asian looking men came asking for Papa's—for Caleb's jade statue. Can you believe it?"

"What did you tell them?"

"The only thing I could. I've never seen anything of jade that could be what they were talking about. So what could I do? I sent them away."

"I can understand that. But who were they representing? Some government ministry? Or just individuals who may be trying to get hold of some very valuable artifacts? We have to be cautious about that sort of thing. They may be feeling things out...wanting stuff to be donated to them, then they sell for the full value."

"I thought it a little strange that they knew exactly what they were looking for, since they seemed to know the story, whether it is true or not. One of then was adamant that a Mandarin had given a statue to Caleb Powel, in payment for taking his mixed race child."

"How did you react?"

"Well enough, I hope. I simply said that if such a thing were true I had no knowledge of it. That my father would not have accepted such a thing. That was not in his interest."

"Were they okay with that? Did they leave a number for you to call, or something we can use to check this out?"

"No—oh, yes. A card with a name and number on it. I don't remember... I put it in the dish on the table in the foyer. I'll get it—"

"Just make sure to have it with you when we leave...I'll be in late tonight, no need to wait up, I have my key. When you are ready we will drive down... it's only a couple of hours drive. Is Millicent coming with us? Well, we can bring her to San Francisco when she's ready."

"Yes, thank you. I *will* be packed and ready to leave when you are. Thank you for coming for me. I could drive, but it is so crowded and unfamiliar...I really don't want to do that."

"I look forward to having you alone in the car, dar—er, Sondy. If I am to get away tonight, I had better cut this off…goodbye, Miss Powell." The dial tone filled the room.

"Until tomorrow, Mr. Everts." Sondy whispered as she replaced the phone. Had he really been about to call her darling? She simply sat thinking about that and a few other things.

Chapter Fourteen

On a Saturday morning in May, Sondra left for San Francisco with Rand Everts at the wheel of a blue 4X4, a two year old Russian Lada Niva. It had two doors and what she later learned was a hatchback at the rear. It had accommodated her belongings with room to spare.

She was rested and resigned to her future in California. She had contacted Trystan Millerson in the office at home in Autumn Village, and she had told him the bold truth. He, of course, nearly panicked until he realized that he was about to receive a promotion to CEO. But she knew him so well that she smiled at his attempt to be serious. She knew that he would leap up, shake a fist and exclaim, yes! Afterward he would return to the serious young man who was married and the father of two children. And follow through with the details she left for him. For now she had her own details to work out.

"Comfy?" Asked Rand. "Need A/C yet? This vehicle does have it."

"It's a lovely day, Rand. Not too hot yet. What an interesting vehicle. It's impressive. We must pay you well."

He grinned, "This is Caleb's. He called it the company car. Whenever we needed to haul something like boxes of paper or some small box or bundle, it was available to whomever needed it. I wanted to be sure we had room for all your luggage. Looks like I guessed right."

"Aren't these cars tremendously expensive? Isn't it foreign made?"

"You don't know Caleb, do you? He told me to find a good used four-wheel drive vehicle for him—maybe a Jeep, or something like it. I found this one on a used car lot… it had low mileage, was only two years old, and the dealer came down to half the asking price in order to clear it out of his inventory. I knew Caleb was going to like that. We've had it a couple of years, now."

Sondra raised her eyebrows at him, "And he didn't question its origin?"

"The dealer didn't know the history because it was a trade in on an American car. As the story went, the former owner was going home to Russia with the new sedan…I took him up on this one right away. Caleb didn't care who made it, it served his purpose. So, no regrets."

"I am finding out more and more about the man Caleb Powell. I am beginning to see why he was successful. I've learned a few things in my business…before I found Trystan. I had a manager for a short while whose major aim was to take advantage of clients who placed their trust in our company. It only took him two months to nearly ruin me. My customers were dismayed at the cheap materials he had used. I nearly fainted when I saw that staggering debt; that is not my way. I fired him, and took over again. I'm not about to put anything in anyone's home that I would not have in mine. Rand, it took months to restore trust again."

"Are you out of debt now? You can easily pay it off with your income from—"

"It's done. I paid off the last five thousand two months ago. I used a bonus check given to me by a family in a small suburb of New York City who, incidentally could afford gratuities. I don't often accept them. Anyway, we are in the green now, and I intend it to stay that way." she smiled over at him; he didn't want her to see his emotion… he quickly turned back to the driving.

For a long way down Interstate 80 neither of them spoke. Then Rand startled her when he asked, "You plan to keep it then?"

Sondra looked out the window as a huge transport pulled up in one of three lanes on their right. She could not see the driver overhead…just his hands on the steering wheel. At least *he* knows where he's going, she thought. I do hope Rand knows how to get over to exit…

"For the time being—" She gasped, "Rand we are over *water*?"

"Oakland Bay Bridge. It is getting on in years, so there are plans to reconstruct it…you don't know that the city is the north end of the San Francisco Peninsula? We'll have to show you what a terrific place this really is; actually, we have a map in the company lobby that tells the story."

"How will I ever have time for sightseeing? From what I have learned of the company so far is that it looks like a full-time job."

"You don't want a full-time job, as you put it?"

"Rand, I am afraid…."

He reached over and took her hand, tightly fisted. He coaxed her fingers to open to his grasp. He held it as long as he could, driving seventy-five miles per hour down a busy eight-lane divided freeway, now over water. "Don't be afraid of anything, Sondra Powell. The people around you are the best. Didn't Caleb Powell choose them? Well, then…"

"I'm not Caleb Powell reincarnated, Rand. I've a great deal to learn, and what if I don't want to be in the import business. What then? Yes, I am afraid." She freed her hand and placed it, relaxed, in her lap.

"Hm. Butterflies. I had those too. The year I went to work for him. I didn't have a clue as to his management style, his personal attitude. Believe me, he didn't pamper me, but it was not painful to find that he did not want a replica of himself, he wanted my talent. That is what he will expect from you. You already understand the import business, and I've seen you thinking about the export side of it too. And now that you know you cannot do it single handed, and that you have the best people already working for you, what's to be afraid of?"

Sondra gazed over at him, watching his hands on the steering wheel. She murmured, "I'm afraid of me. I don't want to lose me."

Rand reached out to cup her face. "I won't let that happen. I, I like you just as you are. You will do fine." He turned to the driving. The sooner they arrived, the better for everyone.

Powell House was first. Rand drove there with ease, to a dismal old Victorian house on two acres of lawn, trees and shrubs. Unusual for the crowded city, but Caleb had planned with foresight. He had bought the place far away from the old warehouse that once housed his offices, in order to keep his family safe and private. It was what Susan had wanted.

But she had never wanted to live at Powell House in San Francisco, to which, in the end, Caleb had retreated, with a married couple living in and tending to his every need. And the city had closed in around his property without invading it.

Now, years later, Sondra gave it her undivided attention as they drove up the curving driveway and stopped in front of another Powell mansion, this one titled Powell House.

Rand announced, "We're here. I know, it is another mansion; Caleb wanted to differentiate…so this is Powell House. Gloomy, huh? I can't wait to see what you will do with this one, Sondra." He laughed and went around to open her door, and hand her out.

The cedar wood siding on the house was painted dark grey, the peeling trim was white, and the worn front door was black. The charcoal colored roof shingles, those remaining, were calling out for help, she thought.

The evergreen shrubs needed a little pruning, the trees were excellent, and some ivy was invading a bow window on the left side, but there it stopped. Not a flower of any color was to be seen. "There is no garage with this one." Sondra murmured as they went up the walk and onto a broad porch. Rand got out the key and unlocked that black door.

"Nope. Caleb let them put a carport of sorts in the back—a little before its time, and that's where he kept his personal vehicle. Not this one. He drove a Ford sedan back and forth to work—so, have you redecorated this one yet?"

"Rand," she squealed, "give me time for goodness sake. And yes. I know what will be done outside." She had to raised her voice, because he was going back to get luggage. He came back with one under his arm, and two pull cases.

"You will have to start with the roof. I noticed some water damage in an upstairs bedroom."

"I have already figured to go for dark blue long-life shingles, and Wedgewood blue for the siding."

He untangled himself from the luggage, "I figured blue was next."

"All that green foliage…"

"So, blue outside. And trim for all those turnings and millwork? Let me guess: white."

"Yes white, but the contrast trim will be a dark salmon. That includes that black door."

He shook his head and started out for more, this time boxes, and he was not surprised when Sondra joined him and loaded up on the clothes protector bags and small articles that would have taken him forever. Soon, they had everything upstairs. Winded and gazing at one another, they agreed. "The kitchen. Coffee." They said in unison.

At Sondra's startled look, Rand laughed, "This way, Miss Powell. Your kitchen is down these stairs and to the right. I have to admit, I cannot wait to see what you will do with this house."

"Better be concerned with what I will do with Powell Imports." She snapped.

"You only make things better, Sondy. I know that now. I have to do something—permit me?" He took her in his arms, again shook his head and placed his lips on hers. And then he gathered her closer as he felt her response. "I've wanted to do that for some time now," he whispered.

She smiled and moved away. "I know. You have tried so hard to keep from calling me darling. Oh, I am not asleep, Rand. That was nice. Now, look at this horrible kitchen. I have my work cut out for me. Do you think," she turned to him with a canister of coffee in her hands, "that Gary Toppel could work on this house too?" she raised her eyebrows at a bakery box on the counter, lifted the lid and said, "Oh, yum. My favorite Danish Rolls. You did this!"

Rand laughed, "Guilty—I think Gary would follow you to the moon now and build anything you wanted there."

"Don't be silly, Rand. Do you happen to know where the coffee maker is? Oh, what's that? A percolator? How do we use it, if you are so smart?"

He showed her, delighted with her. In a house that was so badly in need of care, he stayed with her, helping with the unpacking until late that night. He was even more elated when she insisted he stay in one of the guest rooms. She was not going to spend the night in a haunted house alone. "What could I possibly have to say to Caleb Powell if he should show up?"

"Hi, daddy?"

She threw a shoe at him, "You are no help. Goodnight, Randall."

It was Wednesday, the last week of May when Sondra Gaye Powell took possession of Powell Imports. The Board of Directors, Rafe Barker, Randall Everts, and all department heads were in attendance as she signed the irrevocable acceptance of her inheritance. And the weight of the world settled on her shoulders.

She had chosen a dress in which she always felt her best. It was pale salmon color, two piece knit. It was of simple design, yet exceptional buttons on the bodice and sleeve cuffs gave real class to the design. She'd added pearl earrings and the Lapis ring. Her plain pumps were slightly darker than the lapis ring, and the outfit served her well.

The atmosphere was a bit strained in the Powell Board Room. She had yet to see her very own office; however, she had noticed the Administrative

Secretary, Diana Lupica and quickly reserved judgment. The woman was a beautiful brunette, voluptuous in an expensive red two-piece dress and red stiletto-heel shoes, and was obviously irritated that a woman was moving into Caleb's office with Rand. Sondra frowned briefly, but moved on. *Did she think it should be Rand's now?*

Caleb had inherited the company; moreover, as it grew he adapted the offices to suit himself, and when he thought it expedient, he created his small corporation. Rafe had explained the choices made, and had taken care of all legalities. Fees, taxes, shares of stock which passive investors bought, the creation of by-laws and at that, Caleb had declared himself Owner/Director and taken on Randall Everts as his Chief Executive Officer. Almost a partnership—however unusual *that* seemed to those around them. To Caleb it was a family-owned business and he kept controlling interest; that was the way he organized it, and perhaps it was why he had achieved success. Only Rafe and Rand knew of his intention for his daughter to someday carry on.

The company board was made up of seven heads of departments, with the title Manager for each one. It had been working well for many years, earning the company commendations for excellent business practices. As Sondra absorbed the extent of her inheritance, she knew she would have little to change about any of it. For some reason, she kept returning to the question of adding Exports to the business. Rafe would have to advise her about that, she decided. And other things.

With the board meeting ended, Managers returned to their departments and the wheels hummed once more. Sondra sat behind Caleb's desk that had a brass plaque: *Director.* "I can't feel anything," she murmured, as her gaze found the portrait on the desk and her heart skipped a beat.

Rand swept in, with Diana Lupica on his heels. He dropped his briefcase onto his own desk. "Feeling beat, are we? You did very well, Sondra. There were good vibes all around. Relax, you are home."

Sondra glanced at Miss Lupica in time to see her purse her lips and roll her eyes to the ceiling. Sondra looked back at Rand, who seemed unaware of the Secretary. "Did you need something, Miss Lupica?" She asked as carefully as possible.

Rand looked up, surprised, "What is it, Miss Lupica?"

She carelessly waved a hand of dismissal, "Just checking, Rand. If you don't need anything I'll get back to my desk."

Sondra clamped down on her gasp. She waited.

"I don't recall signing any of the correspondence I dictated. Do you have that ready?"

"Oh, I got those done; I signed for you. They went out last night."

"You did what? Tell me you *didn't* sign my name to those documents. You do not have that authority. You had best get them in here for my signature, and now."

"But I just wanted to help you in this time of awful change. You have too much to do with her here...."

"Miss Powell is the head of this company. This is her office...."

Rand stared at her, and Sondra knew exactly when it hit him. He snarled, "You have overstepped your boundary, Diana Lupica. Your actions are unacceptable. You are an employee—you've stepped out of line. I am giving you two weeks' notice. You need not come in after today's shift end. There is no position for you here. I will give you references, but that's it. Nothing more."

Sondra felt a cold breath of fear as she saw the glitter in the woman's eyes. It was not tears, of that she was certain. The look swung over to her, intensified with a vicious twist of the secretary's lips that turned into a pout, as she turned and hurried out of the office.

Rand swept both hands over his hair at the temple, and took a deep breath, "I didn't enjoy that one bit. Where did she get off signing correspondence in my behalf? She definitely does not have my Power of Attorney. I've no idea what went out of here. For gosh sakes—"

The private phone pealed out and she quickly picked up. "Hi, Rafe. Yes, it is done. I am sitting behind the Director's desk and just remarked that I don't feel anything." She laughed. "All right...yes. I have seen the house. No not restoration, *revival*. The poor thing is dead...yes, I have already decided on the outside colors. If Gary is available, the roof must be done *ASAP*."

Rand could hear Rafe, "What about the inside? Are you going to replace everything? If you can come in under budget again, it will set well with Rand."

"If she's going to live there," Rand raised his voice, "we'll budget enough for whatever she wants." But he was cut off by the intercom as Diana said, "Mr. Everts, there is a gentleman here to see you. Mr. Fowler from the U.K., about some pharmaceutical shipments."

"See that he is comfortable in the lounge. We'll join him in just a few moments."

"We? Oh. Yes. Miss Powell rules now. I'll do as you ask."

Rand snapped off the intercom. He shook his head as Rafe asked, "What the dickens was that about? Was that Diana Lupica? Rand what's going on?"

"I've given her two weeks' notice, she is leaving at close of day."

"What happened? Nothing too serious, I hope."

"Might be, Rafe. She did up some letters I dictated and signed them with my signature…and mailed them. She won't be coming back."

"That's the last we'll hear from her then," Rafe said.

Chapter Fifteen

By Friday morning of that week, Sondra was feeling more at ease with her situation. She had given four hours to her positioning at Powell Imports on Thursday; moreover, a replacement had been found for Diana Lupica, and business went on as usual.

She had contacted Gary Toppel and he assured her that he would pick up shingles and he and Wilford would get that roof done next week. When she was ready for the rest of the work to be done on Powell House, he would relocate and get it done.

"Just get your plans firm, and give me a call. I will follow them to the letter, Miss Powell."

"What happened to calling me Sondra?" she laughed. "We were on friendly terms, then. Not now?"

"Well, now, anyone gets a title of Director of a big company deserves respect."

"So, if I brand you Director of Restoration, you must become Mr. Toppel. I will keep that in mind."

He grunted, "Your aunt sends her best."

"You are at the mansion? What does she have you doing?"

"She wanted a wardrobe closet for all the darned dresses and stuff she has filtered out of the attic. Nearly done. You will like the idea…cedar-lined, thank Gosh. That's better than mothballs…got to go. Take care, Madam Director."

Sondra shook her head, cut the connection, and reached for a folder.

Sue Lee called a little after four p.m. "Sondra, I am free this weekend. I want to shop for a bridesmaid dress for you. Can we have the day together? I would love shopping with my sister. I always dreamed we would one day…It would be wonderful."

"Oh, yes. *Sunny*. I am going to call you that, you are so bright and happy…I'd love shopping with you, more than anything. How—where do we do this?"

"I'll have James drive us so he can drop us off at Union Square. Everything is there…all the great stores. I think Neiman Marcus will be first. They are fab…we'll pick you up about ten tomorrow morning. We can get a cabs to take us home when we are ready—I really like being called Sunny by you."

"I'm glad, Sunny…Nine o'clock in the morning? I like an early start. Lunch will be on me. I think I have comfortable walking shoes. Can you believe I am excited already? What a day that will be."

It truly was a day for them to remember. James, following instructions, dropped them off, and watched them go into the mall without looking back. He shook his head in amazement because he thought them both so darned beautiful. The two women had been dressed in slacks which were almost the same color grey. Sondra had on a blazer of dark red Linen over a silk shell the color of cream, and his darling Sue had chosen a huge green shawl-neck sweater that covered her little rear end. It nearly obliterated her caramel colored blouse.

"Those Powell sisters are seductively gorgeous," he murmured, laughed aloud and sped away to his own responsibilities for the day.

"This is awesome," Sondra quipped, as they went into Neiman Marcus through revolving doors and entered another world.

Sue Lee, holding her right arm close to her chest so as not to attract attention, discreetly pointed upward. "Get a load of that stained glass dome…it is stunning. There's floor to ceiling windows too, looking over Union Square. I always love it here. I think it might be like this if I went into outer space to a new planet." She giggled like a very young girl.

Sondra laughed. "Ethereal, then. I know what you mean."

"Come on, sis. This way to the bridal shop. We have a dozen places we can shop until I find just what we need. You know, Sondy, we have to kind of go period. I can't have you in a spaghetti strap cocktail dress and me in a dress out of the past…it's going to be a challenge. If we don't find it here, I know of a very expensive shop—*The Edwardian Era Collection*—not far from here and we might have to resort to going there."

After three hours of skimming through the wedding sections of several of the big stores, Sue Lee exclaimed, "It's past noon. I need to eat. Let's do the food thing. Where are we? Oh," she grinned, "the chicken here is divine. You said you wanted to treat."

And Sondra did treat, to luscious chicken salad on croissant rolls with a couple of pieces of carrot stick, three olives, and a pot of tea. And blueberry cheesecake the size of a mini muffin, and they had dined sufficiently. And from there they went at last to the amazing Edwardian shop that bought and sold elegant apparel from that era. In only a short time, Sue Lee spied a gown and hat on a manikin that was perfect. The dress was lavender silk *Crepe de Chine*, with lace scarf-bodice which had a high neck, sleeves to the elbow and flared from under the bodice in an exciting look, perfect for Sondra's figure.

"Look at this Sondy. Do you agree we have found your dress?"

"It's gorgeous. What size is this? Yes that's my size—oh, Sunny, we need that hat. I have to have that hat…but *you* won't be wearing one, will you?"

"Oh, yeah. I didn't tell you. I'm not doing a veil…I found a hat when I realized that was the style to go with Hilda's gown from that era. I went to a friend who is in the theater and she had an old off-white velvet thing that looks like somebody made a pot and then squashed it down, trimmed it with narrow burgundy ribbon and pink roses and nested it in light grey gauze. I will undoubtedly be a bride straight out of the nineteen hundred Edwardian era. Move over Hilda, I say. I'm coming in your clothes."

For a fraction of a moment, Sondra felt a chill, but quickly dismissed as a draft.

"Then your maid of honor must have *that* hat." She said emphatically. "I really must insist."

"We want this dress, and the hat, too," Sue Lee told the saleslady standing beside them, and they walked out with the dress in a hanger bag, and the lavender straw hat in a box too beautiful to look at. Broad brimmed and flat at the crown like the Spanish gaucho hat, it was trimmed with a little pink rose corsage on the right side, which anchored the twist of sheer fabric encircling the crown.

As they waited for their taxis, Sue Lee said, "I am going to have the most gorgeous wedding you ever saw. I bet it will scare James to death. But I can't help it. My life is complete now. I can't ask for more than I have. God has been good to me, Sondy. He gave me you."

"Sue Lee. I have to confess. I was wrong about you. But now that I know you and see our love for one another, I think we have so much to make up for that we may not have enough years left…that scares me."

"Well, we aren't going to be separated ever again. No matter where you are in this world, I will be able to call you, and write to you, and someday we will love each other's children—wow. Think of that, Sondy. Our kids."

With that Sondra nodded to the taxi that stopped in front of her, Sue Lee dashed for her cab which had arrived at the same time, and waved from the window as she left, as Sondy was being carefully helped in with her packages.

"There will never be another day like this," Sondra murmured as she was trundled home, feeling anxious to get her shoes off…shopping was hard on the feet, after all. Especially almost eight hours in a city as exciting as New York City. She whispered a strain from a familiar song, "*San Francisco here I come, Right back where I started from…*"

The wedding of Sue Lee Powell and James Kwan, held in the church of his choice, was beautiful, intimate and took an hour, for it was not a ceremony, but a worship service often preferred by Christian couples. Which pleased Millicent exceedingly.

Rafe had deliberately driven, taking Millie with him, amused that she would not fly in a small plane. And he had laughed when they reached Powell House and she had stared at it from the car window, and said, "Good heavens. The place is dead as a doornail. Whatever was Caleb thinking to let it go like this…well, Sondy will also take care of this house."

For the big event, Rafe couldn't help noticing that Millicent was not in her skirt and sweater, but was clad in a tan lace dress and she secured a gray hat with tan trim to her hair which she'd had tweaked a becoming blonde at some beauty parlor…she was one beautiful person, in his estimation. She had endured more heartache than he could imagine. She was the most selfless person he'd ever known, except his own mother. Wallace Sherman had treated her so badly it made him shudder to think of it.

A number of the Chinatown residents were present, since James also had family nearby, and Gem Chang had brought her brother and his wife as friends of the bride. Among them, Sondra thought she recognized one of the men who had come about the jade. But her attention turned elsewhere and she gave no more thought to that possibility. Indeed, she realized, a number of Powell Import employees were right at home at this event. The Manager of Personnel,

Sean Donahue who appeared to know Millicent, hijacked her for the entire evening. Evidently, Sondra decided, many of Caleb's associates *had* befriended Sue Lee, and they seemed to know James as well.

There were friends of Sue Lee's from school days; it was almost impossible for her to get to all of them to introduce her sister, Sondra. She tried during the reception in the Church hall, but later used a microphone and she took time to introduce Sondra to the guests from her personal world. Sue Lee Powell Kwan was a beauty in her bygone days dress; however James, caught up in her happiness, had searched for a few hours until he found striped pants and a frock coat in the same Edwardian shop which assured him that it was the style for the eighteen nineties. Inordinately satisfied tht he was pleasing his love, he purchased a top hat, and placed it on the entry table at the church upon arriving, and set back atop his head as he exited a married man.

"She could not have chosen a finer man," Sondra told Rand. They were at the table with the wedding party, eating cake and drinking lemonade punch and listening to toasts to the bride and groom. Caught up in the emotion of the moment, she found herself visualizing her own wedding to Rand Everts. She moved among the guests easily, visiting with people she did not know and would never recall despite their outpouring of information that they were mostly dignitaries of the judicial system that Sue Lee and James were involved in also.

When it came time to open a few of the presents that were arranged nearby, Rafe moved over to Sondra's side and handed her a black velvet folder. "It's all here. Just as you asked. I got the deed clear in time. I doubt they suspect a thing. We had some good times going around to look at Victorians. They were crazy about this one, didn't know it was for sale, so this should be the best for them. You are generous, Sondra."

Rand moved in close, "You got the place then? That's good. They may be successful, but they're not ready to take on a huge mortgage."

During a lull in package opening, and gathering up wedding paper and ribbon, Sondra stood up and went up to Sue Lee. She wedged in between the couple, held up her hand and said "I have a gift, but it is in a folder. I couldn't afford paper…" She waved a hand at the huge bundle on the floor. "Open this, Sue Lee, and James. Take it with all the love I have to give to the two of you. And with the promise that I will babysit sometimes when the family comes… as will my co-partners in this, Randal Everts and Rafe Barker."

The room erupted in more laughter and then stilled as Sue Lee opened the folder, looked at James and handed it to him. For a moment he looked puzzled and then he looked up at Sondra and said loudly, "You have got to be one crazy woman, and two crazy men."

Sondra bent down and kissed him on the cheek. "I am—only me. Crazy about the Kwan's. My sister and brother. Congratulations and forever happiness, James and Sue Lee."

"It's a house. Not just any house, but the one we have dreamed of forever. How will it be, Sue, honey? You know, Sondra, you could have bought a set of China and it would not have been as expensive as this."

"You don't need China. Sue Lee has a set that was mother's—at the mansion in Sacramento. Mother left her some special things in trust…as she did me."

"We can never repay you, Sondra."

"Did you see a bill in there? Then I will say this last one thing. If I ever need a place to stay, I know I can come to your house."

James closed the folder and clutched it to his chest. Then he handed it back to Sue Lee and stood up. He pulled his bride up and kissed her, reached down for his glass of champagne and toasted their friends and gift-givers, and drank with everyone.

How fortunate we were, Sondra thought as Rand drove them home. Rafe and Millicent followed shortly and in the fashion of families, they spent an hour discussing the event of the year in their lives. "Hilda's dress was the star attraction, you know." Millicent recalled Susan's rejection of it, opting instead for her little cotton frock. Which, in the end had been the best choice. She turned to Sondra, "Where in the world did you find that dress and hat? You almost stole the show it is so gorgeous. It was just as Edwardian as Hilda's. I know it wasn't in our attic at home."

Looking amused, Rand said, "It took her and Sue Lee eight hours to scour Union Square before they came up with it in a specialty shop."

"It was a most heavenly sister's day on the town, Rand Everts. Don't forget that. We had each other and that was all that mattered."

"But, eight hours to buy a dress?" Rafe groaned. "My feet hurt just thinking about it."

"Oh, Rafe. It wasn't buying a dress for the maid of honor. It was finding each other again and erasing the years we'd been absent from one another. With each garment we inspected, we revealed ourselves. We were alike in our choices, but there were differences that we discovered without fanfare. We fit together like…like sisters of many years."

'Well, my darlings," Millicent eased out of her chair, "is anyone interested in a cup of coffee before we call it a day? No takers, okay. I am going up to bed. I must take off this tight girdle."

Stunned, all eyes were on her. No way did she have on a girdle. And then Sondra began to laugh, the others joined in and Millicent hugged them. She said goodnight and went up to bed.

Rafe had been assigned a guest room when they had arrived. Rand had only to remind them that he had been staying with Caleb for the last few months, and if no one objected, he would bed down in the room the housekeeper had assigned to him. He would lock up and turn out the lights, which he did after their footsteps faded, and the last door closed.

Rand tried to go right to sleep, but the vision of Sondra in her wedding outfit filled his mind, and his heart. It was all he could do during the ceremony to control himself. He wanted so badly to hold her in his arms and take off that hat…He turned over several times, then got out of bed and went to a window. He pulled back the dusty drapes and stood looking out at tomorrow. Could he dream, he wondered, of someday making Sondra Powell his bride?

James and Sue Lee did not honeymoon. They were so smitten with the house which Sondra and Rand and Rafe had given them that they spent almost two weeks moving their individual belongings into place and when they felt content with the look and feel of the house, they settled into domesticity and within days were happy as an old married couple. Before long, James had to travel to Argentina, Sue Lee was facing a full schedule at court and the wedding pictures were all that remained at home some days.

Sondra became involved in Powell House with Gary Toppel. The old roof was gone and the new blue one was the first of the revival. Going in to the office at eight until twelve noon, she would endure the taxi drive, often stopping off at some handy paint store, planning in the cab and at home, until she was satisfied that the worn, gloomy structure was taking on a new personality.

The day she ventured into an outlying fabric store looking for replacement cloth to make the windows and some chairs come to life, she was unaware that she was being stalked. He had been sitting across the street from Powell building, when she claimed the black and white taxi that pulled up to the curb. He simply made an illegal U-turn, and followed at a discrete distance so that he saw her leave the cab and go into store indicating A World of Fabrics.

"Ok," he gritted to himself, "this will be a snap, first she goes to paint stores. Now she picks up cloth to sew with…antique shops next?" He went on down the street and disappeared.

He was not there to see her stop at a lamp shop. She exited with a pair of lead crystal vanity lamps, and this time a redheaded man in a Ford truck picked her up and carried her home.

Sondra reached home after three o'clock, thanked Gary for his help and for the first time she backed Caleb's car out and carefully made her way to Brierley Antique Shop five blocks away. She'd found two wooden rose dogs for the drapery tieback in the den which was nearly done. Parking was at a premium, obviously at the back of the building, and down a narrow lane. She eased into a spot.

There was no rear entrance, so she went round to the front. And with a minimum of conversation, pleasant though it was, she left in minutes with her purchase, complete with hardware for installation, in two square boxes; she stepped out into the waning sunlight and hurried around the building. It was annoying and a bit scary that they had no rear entry. Startled, now, she saw that a sports car was blocking her. A man sat waiting. But suddenly she was worried…no one had come into the store while she was there.

She set the boxes on the top of the car and took out her keys. Before she could unlock the car, the man got out, carrying a bundle of some towels, she thought. He was on her in seconds. She looked into a triumphant gaze and saw amusement. "This was easy, Sondra Powell. But the rest won't be. I don't *want* to mess up a doll like you. Hey, I got nothing against you…just doing what I get paid for."

The chloroform hit, and Sondra slumped into his arms. He put her into the back seat of his sports car, covered her with a blanket and backed out of the parking lot into the street; he drove away smiling.

Sondra's keys were in the car door lock. He hurried back for the two boxes and took them with him.

Chapter Sixteen

Sondra was not allowed full consciousness at any time. After dark, in a rented room not far from where he'd abducted her, he calmly propped her up on a wooden ladder-back chair, and every time she teetered, he used his fists, fitted with men's heavy cabochon rings to slam her back upright. He kept it up until she tried to resist, then he again used the soaked cloth. He dragged her to a bed, threw her on it and left locking the door behind himself. "Gotta get some dinner," he muttered, a little tired. He had left his slippery bloodied rings on a table where he could find them for the next session.

At ten' o clock he returned and looked her over. Most of the cuts on her arms and chest were oozing blood; it seeped through her white shirtwaist. Nodding at her pathetic protest, he started on her abdomen, he pulled off her slacks and worked down her thighs until they were a pulpy mess. When she screamed, he felt his body stir and grinned, but he wasn't interested in a go at her and relaxed as her moans grew fainter. In time, Sondra no longer responded and he was satisfied that it was finished for tonight.

He opened a black lawn bag and took out scissors from the collection he carried in his car. He hacked off most of her hair, which he carefully stuck to her wherever there was blood or any moisture. Boasting loudly in the silent room that he was clever for preventing any way that he could be traced to her. He wasn't going to take any rap for doing *Deedee's* job. "Damn women, anyway. Why can't they duke it out over the guy. Oh, no, they gotta get someone to kill for godsake." He closed the bag, and left with it in his hand.

He returned even earlier on the second day, went a couple more rounds, and even though he was tired, he opened his pants and pulled his excited member out, and played with her until he decided it looked like she would die soon; however, his twisted mind said he needed to let his kin know he had done his job, so he took out his pocket knife and cut the initials D.L. into Sondra's right thigh. The Powell woman would never know what the significance of that was, and if she lived, he'd be long gone…It wouldn't do to stay near that conniving relative of his; she could fend for herself, from here on out.

He tucked himself into his trousers, zipped up and stood staring at her.

Mesmerized, he watched Sondra's blood seep. He didn't bother to blot it. He simply replenished the chloroform, held it to Sondra's face, and when he was satisfied, he threw it aside, dragged her outside to his car and drove to within three blocks of Powell House.

The street was empty. He sat for half an hour, parked, studying the flow of traffic. He got out and opened the back door next to the curb, dragged her body out and dropped it into the gutter. He ran around the car, got in and drove away at a leisurely pace, and lit a cigarette as he hit Interstate 80 east intending to leave California for good. Five thousand dollars would see him set up in Nevada. Deedee could fork out more money when he needed it. He would never be far from *her*.

Five blocks from the interstate exit, a police car pulled him over. He was astonished to learn that someone had been watching out of the window in a two storey house where he had parked. The woman got his license number, called 911 to report he'd left the body of a woman in the gutter. An ambulance was on its way to her, and *he* was being arrested for attempted homicide. He'd get murder one if she died.

The name on his driver's license was Alldo Lupica.

"This is a grisly one. But she'll live." The officer and medic from the ambulance agreed that it was a sickening attack. "Senseless."

"The guy left a trail a mile wide. Why would he throw her handbag out with her, and the two little boxes she must have just purchased…why leave his prints all over everything? Guess we will know pretty soon. It was smooth the way the lady in the house handled everything…well, take care of this one, and get her to hospital. I'll call Powell Imports and report to the CEO. He will know who else needs to be notified, I'm sure."

"Looks like she is trying to come around, we'll get going, officer. Good luck with this case. Sometimes things do go your way, don't they?"

"Sure do, Bryan. Sometimes." He gave a little salute, got into his vehicle, and listened to the report that the man, Alldo Lupica, was in custody in Oakland. "This is one time I am happy to be a policeman," he murmured and left the idling ambulance, which passed him later with siren blasting away. He pulled over, reached for his mobile and punched in Powell Imports.

Rand was just getting ready to leave for the day. When the phone shrilled out in the quiet room, he set down his briefcase and answered, knowing the temporary secretary had already left.

"Mr. Everts, this is officer Marquez, SF police officer. I'm calling to let you know Miss Sondra Powell has been found. She was taken to Emergency at Arden Med Center. You might want to contact her family, sir. I understand there is an aunt, Millicent Sherman…Fine. Thanks. I have no report other than the medic opinion that she is badly hurt, but should make it with good care—Mr. Everts, we got the guy—Mr. Everts?"

Rand Everts had disconnected, Officer Marquez concentrated on getting to the hospital for a check on Miss Powell. It was not required, but he always followed up just the same. After several tries to get Rand on the phone, he gave it up and drove on.

At the medical center, Rand arrived with a police escort and was accompanied to the information desk. In moments a volunteer led them to ER and made contact for Rand. A nurse filled him in, the police escort left and Rand sat down to wait.

In one hour the same nurse accompanied the gurney down the hall with the unconscious Sondra tucked in and tubes helping her stay alive.

"Where are you going with her, nurse?" Rand was up and at her side instantly.

"She's being taken to surgery to repair lacerations and a knife wound. They might have to look at the liver but are guarded, hoping it was only bruised." She moved on, calling over her shoulder, "You can get some refreshment while you wait, Mr. Everts. Has any of her family arrived yet?"

"Her Aunt, Millicent Sherman, will be here sometime tonight. She was on her way back to Sacramento, and has had to be intercepted…I'll be here in any event. Please let me know as soon as you can about Sondy—Miss Powell."

"We need next of kin—"

"Judge Powell! Has anyone let her know? They are sisters…"

"Judge Powell? Sisters? I don't think—"

"Yes. I will contact her immediately," Rand uttered. And the gurney disappeared down the hall.

Before he could gather himself up enough to go make the call, he heard, "Where is she? What have you done with my sister? Yes, Sondra Powell is my sister—not that it is any concern of yours, but I was adopted. Now where is she?"

Rand stood up, "Sue Lee. Come and join me. They just took her to surgery. She'll be okay, they just have to repair of a couple of cuts." As he explained the entire event, Sue Lee became less agitated and together they waited for the return of the gurney. The last twenty minutes were spent in silent fidgeting. Rand could not move, he simply sat numbly and wondered if Sondra had been raped. He wasn't aware of his moan.

It was nearly midnight when Millicent rushed into the room where Sondra was resting comfortably. Rand and Sue Lee were sitting in the dark beside her bed, waiting. Rafe was right behind Millicent as if he had been holding her up. "What has happened to her?" She cried. "Who did this to my darling Sondy?" She brushed Sondra's hair back and kissed her puffy face. "Oh, honey, no."

Again Rand went through the facts. "I think the officer said they got the guy who did it. I can't be sure. We have been too concerned about Sondra. I'll check it out in the morning…well later, since it is almost morning. But, you have to know she will be all right. She has terrible bruises and cuts, they repaired what they could of a knife wound, and decided not to operate on the liver after all. The doctor said the liver suffered some trauma, but that the organ has the capability of healing and regenerating, so she will be back to normal in a few weeks."

Now Millicent was weeping. "Oh, Sondy honey. I should never have made you come to this awful place. Look at you…even your hair. What a monster to do such a thing to you."

Sue Lee said, softly, "Millicent, you mustn't think like that. Everything happens for a reason. You will see when we learn who did this and why. It had nothing to do with you, I can bet on it. I've been in law long enough to see it all the time…she wasn't raped the doctor said. So, he may have been watching her because he thought she had lots of money to shop for all that stuff she was collecting for the house. You'll see, dear Millie, You'll see."

Sondra had opened her eyes and in the dim light saw the silhouettes of people and realized they were gathered around her bed. "I am in the hospital...did they catch that man?" Her voice dropped to a whisper, "I was helpless; he kept smothering me with a towel, but it didn't work." She moaned and before anyone could respond she had gone back into her medicated slumber.

The door opened, the light brightened and a nurse said, "Where did you all come from? Are you all family? Really she should not have so many of you in here. She needs to be kept quiet for a few hours. Her mother may stay, but the rest of you must wait out in the waiting area. I'm sorry. Doctor's orders..."

They all filed out. "But, I said her mother could stay..."

"Do you mean me?" Millicent said. "I raised her. I am her aunt."

Through the open door they heard Sondra's faint call for Rand. He looked surprised, as they all did, but he went back to her bedside. "I'm here, Sondra. What is it, what do you need?"

"I hurt so badly." It was a hoarse croak, "Please stay, unless you'd rather not."

"But your sister and Millicent are here—?"

"You. Please, just you."

From behind him, the nurse said, "I'll send the others home for the night. You can use the recliner, Mr. Everts, and stay with her."

"Okay. Yes, I'll stay Sondy. I'm here. Go to sleep now."

Sondra closed her eyes. The others left, promising to return later, and Rand made himself comfortable as the nurse dimmed the lights and the hospital grew even more silent.

Once, in the night she stirred and Rand waited. But when she grew still, he stood up and leaned over her. He feathered kisses on her temple and adjusted the covers and sat back down,

---

Sondra remained in the hospital for a week, and then was transferred to a nursing home for continued care for another week. She was amazingly resilient in the face of the bruises on her body and damage to the liver. The surgery healed nicely after a battle with a bit of infection. The obvious scar had now taken on its true identity as it healed in a thin red line. But it was only weeks later that they were able to put together the symbols, D L. All the stitches had been removed.

Rand, having learned the identity of Alldo Lupica had gone to the police and discussed what connection, if any, this man had to Diana Lupica, a former employee whom he had fired for insubordination. When the connection became obvious—the two were brother and sister—Diana was apprehended as she was attempting to get on a plane. No amount of denial on her part was acceptable in view of Alldo's confession and the two were arraigned without bail for the attempted murder of Sondra Powell.

Those days were extremely hard on Rand. His duties at the company kept him away from Sondra when he knew she was needing for him to be nearby. The liver's flu-like symptoms began to abate in a couple of weeks, and the doctor decided she could return home, but some nursing care would be required, perhaps a visiting nurse several times a week. Because he was training a new secretary, he couldn't spend as much time with Sondra as he would have wanted to. She seemed to cling to him…and he could not take advantage of her neediness to be more than a brother, or friend. Rand Everts knew for certain that he was in love with her. The question was, did Sondra return that love, or was this tenacity of hers something else? He could only hope.

Millicent went back to Sacramento two days before he took Sondra home to Powell House. The roofing job was finished, and Gary was waiting for the next project, so Millie needed to get back to her renovation of that attic. Sondra's recovery was almost complete.

With new storage cupboards and wardrobe closets it was shaping up. Millie was looking forward to commandeering that freed-up space for her work room. She loved needlework, this was the ideal place to spend time in the old rocking chair she'd discovered, and the idea that she could now begin to paint gave her a nudge in that direction. Toppel was helpful, he would redo the dormer windows for more light, and with a coat of paint she would be in business.

Sue Lee arranged to spend the first week at home with Sondra. She was concerned that Sondra clung so tenaciously to Rand Everts. What was going on? Surely she would not react like that after abduction by a man and such a beating. But, "Things are never what you think, James. I just cannot figure this one out. I have seen so much trauma…this doesn't fit the bill."

James, the perfectly content husband, had merely shrugged and agreed. To him the violence that resulted from Diana getting fired from her job was not the true picture, either. That woman had to have some other motive. Could hatred and jealousy be reasons for wanting someone dead…enough to actually carry through with it? "Don't worry your mixed-race brain, my wife. Just go to your friend, but for a few days. After that you're mine again."

"You are silly, James. I am yours every minute of every day, forever. Don't forget that you handsome hunk of a man."

"Well, Beautiful Willow, I can't possibly come over to the house and make love to you."

She leaped into his lap, and for a few moments they belonged to each other, exclusively.

"I've got to go, James. I love you. Call me, okay. I imagine Sondy sleeps a lot yet."

"Oh, well, if she sleeps a lot, maybe I could come over after all…"

"Husband." She kissed him, "behave. I'll see you tonight, after she's settled."

"You gonna leave her alone all night?"

She looked at him, considering. "No. Rand is staying in the house with her. We aren't broadcasting that. It's nobody's business, but there are those who will make it theirs…"

"Why is he there? Have they got a thing going?"

Sue Lee frowned, "I'm not sure. I believe he is in love with her. But I can't figure out why she has clung to him like she has. Well, I guess we will know one day."

James watched her gather up her things, and leave. He was head-over-heels in love with her, and he had been inordinately pleased to learn she had not inherited a fortune from Caleb Powell. He would not have wanted to be branded a kept man. "Not even love would have made me endure that," he muttered to himself. He looked around at the house that had been their wedding gift and was happy about that. He grinned. It would even accommodate a couple of children one day. He went to his desk and sat down. He had a ton of work to take care of. Better get to it.

When he thought Sondra could handle some decision making, Rand approached the subject of her plans for housekeeping help. The couple who had taken care of Caleb were retired, both too infirm to do the work any longer. So, did she want a professional cleaning service weekly, or to search for individuals who actually liked housework.

"I prefer to call them Domestic Managers. A live-in pair, or a couple of women or even one woman if she is capable of handling it all…that would be ideal. But I don't know anyone with a Degree in anything who is going to wait tables or cook and clean…actually, Rand I was thinking of asking Alma if she knows anyone…let's see what she has to say."

What Alma had to say was that she sure did know someone, her cousin, Mavis Griffin in Oklahoma needed work. She had been alone too long. No children, she had married Lou Griffin, but after ten years he had left her for another woman. "It took her awhile to digest that, I can tell you. There was a Senator friend of the family who convinced her to work for them. She became a part of the family, you know. Rand, she had it so good…darned if he didn't get indicted one day for something or other, and that family fell apart. Mavis was out of a job…hasn't worked like that since. Scared to try, I guess." Alma was making cookies and moved the batter away from Rand.

"Would she come out to California?"

"Sure. I'll talk to her. If she'll stay, fine. If not, we're only out plane fare."

Alma bent to put the cookie sheet in the oven, and Sondra wanted to laugh, because Rand had jabbed a finger in the dough and stuck a blob in his mouth. He was on the way back for another, when Alma straightened and moved the bowl.

"No, no, little boy. Get outa my cookie dough. I'll have a baked one for you in a minute."

"Busted!" admitted Rand Everts. "Okay, ladies. Let's get Mavis here as soon as possible."

"So then, let me tell you how we're gonna handle Mavis—" Alma advised.

"Mavis needs handling?" asked a startled Rand Everts.

"Goodness yes. She's never been outa Oklahoma. Always worked too darned hard. Husband left her to fend for herself…She'll need us to show her the way."

Chapter Seventeen

Mavis Griffin did not get handled, she did the handling from the minute she arrived at Sacramento International Airport, grabbed a skycap to help her with four large pieces of luggage while she carried her purse, a shopping bag and her overnighter, in search of her cousin Alma.

Alma warned Millicent and Merilee, "in that shopping bag she's got leftover lunch stuff, her knitting, and a book, apples and a bottle of water, package of trail mix, and a pack of licorice. She's the worst person I ever knew to fill up a paper bag with stuff she wants handy. And it's only three hours and forty-five minutes on United. Bet she never touched a thing in that bag."

By the time they got to the car, the only thing left in the bag was her knitting and book. She'd put the lunch debris in the trash bin in the airport, given the skycap the treats and watched him walk away smiling as he tore into them, after unfolding a couple of dollar bills.

No one laughed. They all recognized that the tall, gray haired woman with soft brown eyes and a gentle voice knew exactly what she had done. It was what she had to give in addition to the two dollar gratuity that was all she could afford. Instead they took a closer look at the woman in her neat black knit dress with a sheer white scarf draped around her neck and held by a black enamel scarf pin, and unassuming black pumps and a huge over-the-shoulder handbag.

Only Millicent was quick to note her misshapen hands that were reddened from work, and her heart went out to this woman whose life was so similar to her own.

Mavis remained in Sacramento for a couple of weeks. She wasn't eager to be exposed to too much of California at once. Getting into the attic with Millicent was fun for her. She liked the window seat the contractor Gary had fashioned, so she got busy making some cushions for it. They were tidy, attractive in the rather plain room, and Millicent asked her to use a couple of drapes salvaged from one of the bedrooms, to make pillows for the bed there.

In time there were confidences that neither of them wished to share with anyone else, having reached a trust found only occasionally in one's life. Hadn't they each been through the ultimate of embarrassment—failed marriages that must have been their fault? In confidence, Millicent told the story of Caleb's life. She avoided the legend of the jade, but the alert Mavis decided that something like a lacquer box was probably payment. "They all have one, and keep little bits of hair or a bone, or a stone as their prized possession."

"Apparently there was no payment, Mavis," Millicent said firmly.

Having gotten over that barrier, Mavis asked to do some cooking so that they might judge if she would be what Miss Powell in San Francisco was expecting. Alma stayed at her side, taking note of some of the little tricks Mavis had of making food so delicious. Merilee, in turn, said "Mavis, you will never be a servant in Sondra's house. You are going to manage everything."

Undaunted, Mavis handled all this information with patience, and did her best to prepare for the interview. Miss Powell could not come to her, there had been some sort of attack and the woman was not able to travel yet. So, the lawyer, Rafe would drive her to San Francisco on a Friday. She could spend the weekend, and wait for a decision. "Let it be me," she prayed.

Thursday morning, no one was downstairs when Mavis went to get herself a cup of coffee. She was sleeping so much sounder and longer in this house. It was the feeling of security that she knew was at the root of it. Being alone could make a woman insecure, could wake her up at odd times at night…she stood looking out the bow window, sipping. She heard the doorbell ring twice.

"Someone get the door, please. I am indisposed at the moment, and Merilee is not dressed." Alma called out from her suite.

"Well, if I must," Mavis murmured, and set her cup on the counter.

The frosted glass in the door was no help. She had to open the door. And when she did, "Oh my God!" she said, and almost shut the door on the two men standing there. She had never been in the presence of a Chinaman as she had heard them called. They didn't seem to be dangerous, they were dressed like two businessmen…they must be from San Francisco, since that is where most of them lived, wasn't it?

"We are making a return visit to Miss Sondra Powell. Would you give her our card and ask if we can trouble her with more questions, please."

"You know Miss Powell? I'm sorry. She is not here. She makes her home in San Francisco, now."

"And Judge Powell. Is she perhaps at home? We could ask our questions of her."

"Too bad you went to all this trouble, but you will find Miss Powell in San Francisco. She will be at Powell Imports—you know that place? You must go there. I have no idea who or where Judge Powell is."

The speaker conceded, "Very well. We will do as you say."

She stood watching as they hurried out to a sleek car at the curb, and drove away. "Well, glory be." She marveled.

Mavis looked at the card in her hand. It was official looking. She placed it in the lacquer bowl and went inside to find Alma working in the kitchen.

"Who was it, Mavis? What did they want?"

"What would two Chinamen want with the Powell women? One of whom is a Judge? Powell's are important people. I am intrigued. Employment will be very interesting, but I don't know how I will feel about foreign people in my life. I have much to learn, I know."

"Well, you will do fine. Stop worrying. For your information, Judge Powell was born in China. She is Chinese and English. Caleb Powell adopted her and raised her in the care of a beautiful bi-lingual woman named Chang. Miss Sondra Powell was raised by…but sit down and drink your coffee while I fill you in. I can see you need to know what you are getting into."

"Oh, not something bad. I hope you didn't get me out here—"

Alma snapped, "Don't get your dander up. Sit, and listen. It will help you see what a fine place this is because the people are great."

Mavis listened and sorted with experience. She was ready to go get her job. She could take good care of Sondra Powell's home.

Rafe was leaving for 'Frisco on Friday and taking Mavis with him. He rather liked the old girl. She'd obviously had a rough time. And he was tickled to see that she and Millie had become good friends; moreover, awareness of the relationship to Alma wasn't going to affect his judgment of her. It was up to Sondra now. He'd drawn up a simple contract at Sondra's instruction but had to tighten up a bit, or she would have given Mavis too much control too soon. Those two houses were costing Powell Imports, but it was work that needed doing. Caleb had not maintained the properties, and now Sondra was doing the job. He had to give her credit…she knew how to stretch a dollar.

It was a pleasant enough couple of hours in the car with Mavis, they exited the freeway about halfway, had a sandwich and coffee at a little place he knew and liked. She was pretty adamant that people were going crazy with food fads. A little bit of everything, and not so darned much gorging on food and folks might slim down. But you had to use stuff that wasn't treated with anything, which was being done in the name of money…why, she had never seen such big fruit in her life. "And wasn't it tasteless, though…?"

She kept up her conversation most of the way, and Rafe realized that time had passed so quickly, he was so engrossed in what she was saying that he almost passed Powell House. It was now freshly painted. "Wow. That blue is the perfect color for the house," he said. "She's done it again. Value now doubled. Man, oh man."

"This is it? This is where I will work, if she'll have me? Gosh all Friday, that is one big expensive place. I had no idea…how many people live in that house?"

Rafe started to name them off, but realized that only Sondra was at home twenty-four seven. The others were in and out…oh, oh. Bet that wasn't going to set with Mavis…

There were workmen all over the place, painting, repairing, taking a piece of furniture to be repaired or restored with new fabric and finish…he had never know anyone who had been able to do the things Sondy was into. Most people just threw stuff away and bought new. But then, she had said, some of the antiques were made of expensive hardwood that was not to be wasted. It could last for centuries. Now, Rafe concentrated on parking and getting Mavis inside without having to jump over sawhorses. They had to avoid a delivery van unloading a settee that was brand new…but he knew better. That was the one in the parlor, he recognized the style that Sondra had called rococo and whistled. The new fabric was stunning.

"Look at that settee," Mavis exhaled. "That would cost a fortune…side chairs too!"

Rafe laughed, "You are in for a surprise, Mavis. Sondy merely sent the old set out to be recovered. That one has been in the house for nearly thirty years."

"Is that right. My, my."

Weaving their way inside, they came upon Sondra in the parlor directing the deliver boys where to put the settee. Rafe had to catch his breath. The room was amazing. "It's the same, but it isn't," he said inanely.

"Do you like it, Rafe?" Sondra smiled at him.

"I think I'll go home and pack and move over here. Could I have a suite upstairs? I could even set up and work from here."

"We have plenty of room. So is this Mrs. Griffin? I am happy to see you. Please come on into the kitchen. They are finished in there and we can have our interview, then get you settled in a room that is completed."

"Mavis," Rafe remembered his manners, "This is Miss Sondra Powell. She will have a good job to offer. So, I'll go out and bring in the luggage. You two get on with it. Oh, Sondy, here's my brief case. The contract is in there…"

"Will the job be in this big house, Miss?"

"Why, yes. As Domestic Manager you will have a cook and a couple of other helpers to supervise, somewhat. Can you handle that?"

"A Domestic what? I thought it was housekeeper—oh, my gosh. This kitchen is beautiful. Mr. Barker said you were restoring the place. What was it like before?"

"The entire house was dark and depressing. But the quality of everything is not to be found these days, so I have just changed some wall coverings and fabrics. It lightens it up very well, don't you think."

Mavis shook her head. "They said you have a business back east, Interior Decorating. I can see that you are good at it, Miss."

Sondra gestured to tea on a tray, with little sandwiches and small cakes. "Chef Sung prepared refreshments for us. We can sit over here, Mrs. Griffin."

Mavis said, "Your cook is a foreigner? Does he cook, that is—?"

Sondra said, "Allen is Chinese American. Born and raised here. He is a chef…and a friend of my sister, Sue Lee. We were fortunate to get him to work for us, he has a position with a big hotel, you see. But he comes here and prepares meals, does the shopping, then returns to the dinner hour at the hotel. With the help of a young single mother, Christie Allred, we do fine. She lives in. Her rooms are through that door, and yours will be there, too."

"Well, I never. I did hear that there's a town for them…."

Sondra, in the midst of serving a couple of little sandwiches, halted. "Do you have a problem with that, Mrs. Griffin? Yes, some Chinese people are more comfortable in a close community—you have to understand that my sister is half Chinese and half English. She is married to James Kwan, and they both frequently spend time with me. They have their own home in San Francisco. We really do have a loving relationship."

"But, but, how—I mean. Oh gosh. I don't mean anything. I just don't know where I will fit in all of this."

Sondra sighed. "Enjoy your tea, Mrs. Griffin. And I will tell you all about us. It will take a little time. Then I have a copy of the contract for you and you can decide in a day or two if you want to stay. I really would like to have you. Alma is a dear person in our life. But I will understand if it isn't what you are looking for."

Within two hours, tea was cleared away, luggage brought in, and a tour was taken of the house under construction, as Rafe had put it. He had snacked, then gone on to the office for a session with Rand. They had some new overseas contracts to adapt. A government agent was due in this afternoon to look them over…in parting he had said, "You are looking pretty as ever, Sondra. I am glad for that—it is over."

"Yes. Me, too. I'll return to work Monday, Rafe. We should be finished here within the next two weeks. Oh, Rafe—have you learned anything about the two men seeking the jade?"

"No luck, Sondra. Can't find a trace of them. That card had a phone number on it, but it belongs to some retired couple in Alameda. So…no. Sorry."

Mavis stirred, "Are you talking about two Chinese men who came to the house in Sacramento last week? They were wanting to visit Miss Powell again, they said. They gave a card to have her call…I put it in that dish in the foyer. I sent them to the office. Did I do right?"

"Okay, Mavis…Sondra, call Sac and have them give you the number on the card." Rafe advised. "We'll try again. The first card we checked out was not printed in the US…no fingerprints but yours. Maybe we'll get lucky with this one. Got to go. See you at dinner."

The room was quiet for a moment. Sondra could smell the roses in a vase nearby.

"You did very well, Mavis." she assured. "May I call you by your first name? I will be Sondra to you. And you need to take this afternoon to unpack a few things…until you decide if you will stay or not. I hope you will stay—please, be comfortable while you consider it."

"Why, yes, I'd like that. Thank you."

Dinner was a festive occasion with Gary and Wilford present in work clothes, Powell Import's owner and execs in shirt sleeves, and Alma, Christie and Mavis sitting down at the dining room table sans aprons They were doing justice to Allen's meal of breast of chicken in cranberry sauce with trimmings, in a brighter dining room with everything the same—yet not the same. There was laughter, and serious talk about the trial of the Lupica's, there was definitely interest in Mavis and Oklahoma, and Rand who sat next to her was careful to interrogate her without being obvious.

Mavis studied the people around the table. They were people she could appreciate. They were all working people, it didn't matter if they were rich or poor. They were friends. She liked that. And she made her decision, which she put off for two more days. There was a sister to meet.

Mavis was fine with the job. She could do the work easily. She knew how to manage a budget, didn't she? The funds she'd manage for this house were far more than her own income but she could do it. She didn't judge Christie, the girl was sensible, hardworking and raising a little boy who was at present with his grandparents in Hawaii for two weeks. Christie did the beds, and tidied up each day, she served Allen's delicious food and sat to eat with everyone most of the time.

"I've got a bit of heaven here, I believe." Mavis whispered to herself. "Maybe. We'll see. Sometimes things aren't what they seem at all."

Mavis was eager for Sunday to come around. The house was pretty well done, except for moving some things around to suit Sondra. That Gary contractor was like the family. He and Wilford actually did the work for her. Mavis had to laugh, Sondra always had a tray of snacks and juice for them. And even more surprising was that Wilford. He could sing like any professional opera star. She loved it when he belted out some one of the oldies she loved. To sing like that when you have such pain, he must be the bravest veteran in the world, she decided.

Sondra carefully considered Mavis. Aunt Millicent had liked her. But something troubled Sondra. This woman might be hiding her prejudice. I can't subject Sue Lee and James to that.

In the end, Mavis was won over by Chef Allen Sung who never saw an enemy in his life.

Now if she could see her way to the more intimate relationship of the two girls….she needn't have worried. Sue Lee and James came to Sunday dinner bringing a decadent desert from *Little Greece Tempts* specialty shop. Yogurt, fat free cream, fruit and bits of granola with nuts. Sue Lee insisted on dishing it up when dinner was over and that won points with Mavis, who had watched her constantly. When Mavis had visibly relaxed, Sondra knew they had won her approval. Especially when Mavis breathed, "I just love that couple."

Dinner over and everyone wandering off for a quiet time to themselves, Rand said, "Come with me, Sondy. You haven't been out of the house for days. Time for a walk along the beach…are you interested?"

"That's the best offer I've had lately…considering."

"I may have something better to offer…later. Get a scarf and sweater, my love."

Sondra did not miss the endearment. Did he know he's called her his love? Her heart actually skipped a beat and she hurried to get her things.

Chapter Eighteen

Rand drove carefully to a place up the coast that had a little cliff-house café on the overlook. A trail and steps wound down to the beach. The breeze was cool, the ocean was lapping at the shore, and there were few people out on this Sunday afternoon. He held her hand going down the steps and did not relinquish it when they turned to walk up the pale packed sand. Almost instantly a glare flashed up into his eyes. He stopped, bent down and retrieved a polished bit of jasper. It was translucent blue, delicate and he started to replace it, but instead put it in his coat pocket. The ocean was being more than generous today. What he'd found was the stone of strength and courage. He had plans for it. *A dinner ring of white gold and diamonds…*

"What was that, Rand?"

"A rare piece of chalcedony, I think, polished by the sea. This is more like a quartz, blue and beautiful, but this has no grain…it is perfect."

"That's biblical…do you like doing this, walking on the beach looking for treasure?"

"Not usually. I brought you here because I have something I want to say. Now I wonder if I *should* say what I want to say. Maybe I don't have the right…"

"Rand. For goodness sakes. What are you being so—so secretive about that no one should be around to hear?—Rand are you trying to tell me you are in love with me, or…"

He stopped, and growled, "No I'm not in love with you. *I love you.* There's a difference. Now what have you to say about that? I know…I know, you have everything, you don't need some poor male in your life to complicate it further."

"Well, I—"

"Oh, hush." He stepped up, enfolded her in his arms and held her. "I don't want to know if I haven't a chance with you. Just let me hold you. You don't have to say anything. I do love you Sondra, but I'd like to hope that someday you might return—"

"Now it's your turn to hush, Rand." She lifted her hands to his face and held it. She held her mouth for him to kiss, and after gazing into her eyes, Rand took that offer.

The ocean breeze caressed them. Rand lifted his head, and she said, "I never knew much about men…I dated one in college who loved…himself. It hurt for a while, but I realized that he was driven to become a surgeon, and had no time for what I wanted from him. What I feel for you is a sense of completeness…is that right to feel? I am complete with you. And I must say I learned that I am safe with you. You won't give me away, will you? I can never stop loving you."

"Oh Sondy, I don't deserve you…"

"Too bad. You are stuck with me. For the rest of our lives."

They stood on the beach quietly holding each other. "It is almost a holy time," Rand said.

"Yes. It is a holy time Rand. I know God is pleased with us, since I believe it was His wish for us to find each other."

"Looks that way to me, too, my darling. I don't want to go back yet, let's walk a bit. Too bad we don't have a dog…"

"Randall Everts! How can you say such a thing…?"

"Wait, wait. We need a dog and a couple of kids to walk with us on the beach, don't we?"

"I think you are going to have to wait for that to happen. For now, I am all you have to keep you company. First things first, Rand."

"Well, yes…will you marry me, my love?"

"Of course. Then we get the dog and children. Can you handle it?"

"I suppose I can work on that."

"I'll help you," she whispered.

The San Francisco International Airport was teeming with activity when Sue Lee dropped off James. She parked, and hurried back to join him. He'd

Papa's Jade

checked his bags through to Argentina and was waiting for her. He folded her in his arms, "I hate this. But a week is needed to get this set up. I have never worked so hard on a project…I can't fail those children, Sue Lee. I only wish you were coming along. You could have a little vacation from your heavy responsibilities. It would be a great chance for you see some of the world."

"James, you will be in meetings. I would have to go alone…when I vacation I want it to be with you, someplace where we can enjoy things together. I really am not into going anywhere without you. So get your job done, get them safe. I'll wait for you, husband. You are mine. Remember that and come home to me. That's an order."

"Yes, your honor. Okay, they are calling my plane. You be careful and lock up when you are home alone. I want to know you are safe, too. I love you, Sue Lee."

"I love you James Kwan."

She watched him until he was gone from her sight. She sighed, feeling diminished for some reason. He is only going for a week, she thought. He is still yours. And on that note, she went for her car and headed to the office. She had a couple of challenging cases to consider and she wanted to get over to see Millicent, and a young friend had asked her to meet a happy father. She had seen through the testimony of the boy's accuser and acquitted him of all charges. Her judgment proved sound, the girl finally admitted she lied… "Ah, people," she whispered and parked in her designated spot and went inside to work.

Sue Lee did not notice the sleek black sedan a few cars away and the two men inside it who were intent on her arrival and progress to the elevator. And neither did the guard.

"Hi, Judge Powell. Got him on his plane, on his way? He's some fine fellow."

Sue Lee knew the courthouse guard, Jake Willis. She was relieved to hear his voice. The vast expanse of vehicles in the poor lighting seemed rather eerie today.

"Yes, thanks Jake. He's in the air by now. For me, it is business as usual. I'll see you on the way out, probably."

"Yes ma'am. I'll be here till eight tonight. The place has a new night man…they do keep hiring. Nobody likes that shift or the graveyard one either. But we got folks in this building doing their work all night long…Need to keep them safe…you have a good day."

Sue Lee thanked him, and went up the elevator and began a day at court. Without James.

At the same time, Sondra, at the office already, was getting more and more involved with the import business. Rand religiously included her in every aspect of the business, and she was excited when he challenged her, "We need to go to Taiwan, Sondra. If we are to renew our contract with them, we need to take a look at their production. Sometimes their quality control is a little slack and bringing in computers and electronics that are faulty causes our consumers to put the blame on us. We should be there for about a week at the most. I will set up the trip—are you far enough along on the house that you can get away?"

"With nearly seven thousand square feet to bring to life, this revival will take a little longer. I am having to search for places to do reupholstering, refinishing and all that. But Gary is finally with me, not trying to do his own thing, and I don't have to worry that he won't follow my plans. I could probably make the trip. It would be interesting to meet our customers."

"Do you wish to choose the date? All right. I'll see to the reservations and make arrangements for the two of us to travel next week…Wednesday to Wednesday so that we can have a weekend to maybe do some sightseeing. It is quite beautiful there."

"That will be fine." Susan closed the folder of correspondence that had required her signature beside Rand's. She got up and took it over to him. "You are next on these. Mrs. Cheney does a great job. Glad we could find someone so quickly. And now, I am going to get home to some chores I want to see to… we've saved another bit of velvet and I may have just the place for it."

"I'll see you at dinner, then?" Rand got up, came around the desk and wrapped his arms around her. But before he could get in his kiss, Mrs. Cheney blasted over the intercom, "Which one of you is expecting Mr. Thorpe? He says he is here from Switzerland…"

"That will be me, Mrs. Cheney. Miss Powel is leaving for the day. Send him in, please.'

The kiss was swift and sweet. "Goodbye, my heart."

The door opened, Sondra waited to be introduced to Liam Thorpe, excused herself and gathered up her handbag and left the two men waiting for coffee. Mrs. Chaney was at her desk, so Sondra went to the kitchenette and prepared a tray. Judith Cheney stood up and took the tray from her, "I'll get this, Miss Powell. I don't blame you for leaving. Must be dull having to discuss pills and how they are made and shipped…"

"Thanks, Mrs. Cheney. No, not dull at all, important. Mr. Everts can handle that. I have obligations elsewhere at the moment. Thank you for taking this in to them. I will see you in the morning."

"Yes, ma'am," Judith Cheney said.

Sondra waited. Their Secretary was five months pregnant, and had just today begun to wear maternity clothes. Unlike mothers who wore tight knits, it was refreshing to see that she had the good taste to wear an attractive frock that was appropriate for the business office, even though her condition was obvious. Sondra smiled and went to the elevator. "Now that is class," she said.

At three o'clock that afternoon, Sondra was at home in her jeans and old shirt when Mavis came looking for her in an upstairs bedroom where she and Wilford were cleaning up after doing the wallpaper. "Ooo, that's pretty," Mavis approved as she stepped in. "Sure makes a difference in here. Makes everything look new, I'd say."

Sondra wiped her hands of the stickiness, "Wilford and I thank you, Mavis. We'll be down for some break time in a minute. Do you have anything good, today?"

"Gingerbread cookies, Miss. And ice tea?"

Wilford grunted. "Gallons of that tea, and about four of those cookies, Mavis."

"Do you need a sandwich first, Wilford?"

"Naw. Not that hungry, honey." He went out wiping his hands.

Mavis looked startled. "Oh. Oh, I just remembered, you have a caller, Sondra. A lady says her name is Eveline Trimble. She said she was Lana Jo's sister and needed to talk to you."

"Lana Jo? But that was—all right, Mavis. I'll be right down."

There wasn't time to change clothes. But she could tidy up her hair and wash off some grime. Whatever could that woman want with her?

Refreshed she started down the stairs and met Wilford.

"I can finish up here, Miss Powell."

"Thank you, Wilford. When my visitor is gone, I'll be back...."

Sondra went down to the parlor and stepped inside. The room was new and beautiful. But not a stick of furniture or artifact had been replaced. The oak was rich and had the patina of years of hand-rubbing oil into the grain. The new fabrics and wall covering were lighter than the original, and like the Sacramento house, it was the same, but different.

Sondra was surprised to see that the woman whom she knew had been Rand's sister-in-law was slovenly, her oily hair was apparently unmanageable, and Sondra felt pity for the scared face. Acne could be horrible to deal with. She adjusted herself in the side chair, and a sour odor filled the air. Their eyes met, and Sondra felt the thrust of severe passion coming from her.

"Miss Trimble. I'm Sondra Powell. I can see that Mavis has brought you refreshment. I am sorry you have had a wait. As you can see I have been—"

"I'll get right to the point, Miss Powell," she interrupted. "I came here to warn you about Rand Everts. He's not what he seems. I know it well…he was married to my sister and he abused her something terrible. We didn't know until she came home saying she had Multiple Sclerosis. It was a cover up of what he done to her."

"Why on earth would Rand Everts treat anyone like that? He is an honorable man. I understand he paid all expenses during her stay at home with her family. You must be mistaken."

"I was her sister. I know. See, he has a woman, a lover, and he's tied to her…always has been. Her name is Selena Womack. She's older than him, but he still spends a lot of time with her. Even now, he is meeting her at the Marriott in Oakland. If you don't believe me, just call over there. They will tell you it's true."

"Why are you doing this? What will you gain by this accusation?"

"We got a lawyer. He's looking into what we are telling him. May put him in prison. It's where he deserves to be after all he done to her."

Sondra swallowed her pain. "And what?"

"We figure he is worth plenty. Maybe get a settlement for our grief, say a million or so."

Sondra laughed, "I happen to know Rand Everts total worth, and at present he is not going to settle anything for millions. You are a fool, Mrs. Trimble. Now, if you will. Please leave. I have more important things to do than listen to this."

Eveline stood up, angry, "I came here to warn you about him. But I ain't coming back to warn you again—"

"Thank you. I do appreciate that. Good day." Sondra gestured to the door and waited until the scheming female had gone out closing the front door behind her with a bit of force. Again that awful odor filled the room.

Sondra sank down on the settee. She was trembling and nauseated. What in the world was that family trying to do to Rand? There surely was no truth in such a story. He was so gentle and patient with her…but she was the head of a company…there was wealth—if there was truth in this accusation, he would be playing her for… "No, no. I won't believe this about him."

Sondra Powell regained a veneer of control before she left the parlor and hurried to the library and closed the door firmly behind her. She went to the desk, took a deep breath and looked up the hotel…it was a Marriott, yes, there it was. She tapped in the number, was connected immediately to information, and in a few moments her world tipped over and spilled out.

"I am looking for Rand Everts. I've been told he is meeting a lady there. Is he there? It is important to locate him…"

"Why, yes, ma'am. Mr. Everts and Mrs. Womack are on the terrace. Would you like me to call him to the phone?"

"No, thank you. I'll not intrude. I'll see him later. Thank you."

"How do I feel," she murmured. "Oh, God. It hurts. It hurts." She placed her head on the desktop and waited but the tears wouldn't come. Presently she got up and went to the huge window that looked out on a gorgeous garden, newly planted with the beauty she wanted.

And that is where Mavis found her at dinnertime. "You been in here all this time? Must have gotten a lot done. Dinner is ready…Sondra, what's the matter?"

She turned. "Nothing. Like you say, I got a lot done. Dinner? I'll run up and change and join you. Is—is Rand here for dinner?"

"Yes, and Rafe came with him. Seems he came in this afternoon, so he'll be staying over with us I guess."

"Oh, that's great," Sondra breathed a sigh, and went up to change into slacks and a soft knit, light blue tunic. She went down to dinner having added a turquoise lavalier and small earrings which she had hesitated over. Rand had given it to her… 'The eye of God is what it's called, my heart.' He had said.

"No. No." she whispered. "I won't believe that woman. I won't."

The table was completely occupied with what Sondra had come to think of has her family. Christie and Davie Allred added to the company. The boy was tall and blonde, and he wanted to be a doctor like his dad had been. He was at ease among adults, but not obnoxious. Christie and Gary Toppel were in a serious discussion of property she wanted to sell but couldn't afford the repairs necessary to list it. Gary said she should get a contractor who would do the work then get paid after the place sold. Christie said she tried that and the guy said he had to have a note or mortgage to guarantee he got paid after it was sold…Sondra tuned them out, only to wonder later if he would solve everything for them.

Rand studied her from his side of the table. Something was wrong. Something had upset his woman, and he didn't like that at all. He would see her later, find out what it was and give her the date and time of their trip. He could not wait to have her to himself. Away from houses and people and the office "I have never loved so well in my life. Mom was right. I have found her."

Mavis and Christie cleared the table, and everyone began to leave the dining room. Rand started around to Sondra, but was surprised when she turned quickly to Rafe and took his arm.

"Rafe, I need to talk something over with you. Can I have a few minutes of your time?"

"Sure. The library. Okay."

Rand watched them leave together, sighed and challenged Davie to another game of chess. However, after two hours, he excused himself and went up to his own room. Maybe later.

Rafe sat and listened to Sondra relate the story of Eveline Trimble. He shook his head. He wondered where and when they were going to attack. This was appalling. He'd warned Rand to keep all the reports and hospital and doctor files for a good reason. This was it. And with all his heart he wished he might not have to clear Rand with Sondra, that he would be able to capture her love for himself.…

Chapter Nineteen

Rafe was no nonsense and firm. "There's no truth in any of this. I recognized early on—when he came to work for Caleb—that Rand had taken on Lana Jo because of his compassion. I thought he'd been more a caregiver than husband…She was only twenty when he married her. Sometimes she was in a wheel chair, then she would be out and doing well for a while, but it became acute when she was in her early thirties and she seemed not to have remissions any more. He was not about to get rich, with the medical costs of that situation."

"How did he manage, Rafe?"

"His dad had not mortgaged the house, and it was left to Rand, not the wife who was left a bit of cash. Rand mortgaged the house to the hilt. And as far-sightedness would have it, when Lana Jo died he owed almost three-hundred thousand on it. He cleaned it up, and sold it for the appraised value, which covered his mortgage and left him with a few thousand dollars in the bank."

"It is understandable, if he was sometimes angry…."

"He was never angry, frustrated maybe that they couldn't do something for her medically. But he would never hurt anyone in any way. He proved that if nothing else."

"You seem adamant about that."

Rafe nodded and went on, "He said Lana Jo was so sweet and loving, but that family was always after her for money. They thought he was rich… he had very little; actually, he was supporting his stepmother—he calls her mom, by the way—after his dad died of Alzheimer's that ate every last penny of the estate. So, Rand was taking care of both of the women, working as a CPA at night after his day job as Chief Operating Officer of an insurance company."

"Now that his mom has remarried, he only gets to see her when she is in town. She married a Texas rancher, said to be part Cherokee, who doesn't have time to mix a lot. But he is good to her, gives her anything she wants. Rand goes to visit them a couple times a year…she is his mother, his biological mother having died at his birth. The stepmom never had any kids of her own; moreover, she and Rand are deeply devoted to each other."

"I just couldn't believe that Rand would have a cruel bone in his body," Sondra sighed. "I was sick at her accusation. What can they do, Rafe? Can they destroy him through the court system? By declaring him guilty until proven innocent? How can we help him?"

"I'll have to talk to him, and warn him about what they are doing. He isn't going to like it, but I will advise him to stay away from them entirely. I can handle this as quietly as possible. I'll try to get the charges dropped before it even starts. I think I know how to do that."

"No money, Rafe. No money. They must not have money. To try to destroy someone for money is reprehensible."

"We have proof that Rand didn't harm her. I don't know if they are aware of the records over the years… there was her treatment during their marriage, while living in Ohio where Rand worked for the insurance company. She would get strong, then go downhill. But it was her nervous system, not bruises and contusions, and not even emotional damage. He was good to Lana Jo and gave her a great life with him. He took good care of his wife who was not really his wife in every sense."

Sondra was shocked. "Oh, Rafe. If you could only make it go away. I can't bear it if there is one shred of ugliness for him."

Rafe stood up, stretched and reached out to help her out of her deep chair. "I am sure I can take care of this. Don't give up on either of us. It's going to be all right, Sondra. Be patient."

"That won't be hard…to do. I have but one recourse and that is to back away from Rand. I also learned today that he has someone he sees quite often. At a hotel…"

"What? Who told you such a thing? I have never heard him say a thing about another woman. I know his feelings for you, Sondra."

"I don't suppose he has told anyone for some reason. Well, I am going up to bed. Time has gone so fast. I have to clear my head and heart and trust you to get this sorted out. How soon can you get a grip on this, Rafe?"

"I should have something to tell you in the next few days. Don't do anything rash, please."

"No, of course not. However, I am going up to Sacramento to visit Aunt Millie. I leave in the morning, driving up. You can reach me there."

Rafe held the door for her and, declining a bedtime snack, he waited for her footsteps to let him know she was in her room. He switched off the hall light and went up the stairs.

Rafe gave a soft rap on Rand's door, but there was no answer, so he went on to his room, showered and tried again. Still no answer. He tried the knob, and the door opened. The room was empty, the bed undisturbed. "What the devil. Rand? Where are you?"

Rafe closed the door and hurried downstairs to the library. It was dark. He noticed a little light in the kitchen, and went there. It was the light on the range. But on the counter there was an envelope addressed to Alma. He stared at it, picked it up and found it had not been sealed. He swallowed and took out the note. Rand was going to be away for a couple of days. He was preparing for a trip to Taiwan and needed to be packing and finishing up some documents to take along. Would Alma please let the others know; 'Thanks. I'll call tomorrow. R. E.'

Rafe breathed a sigh of relief, carefully replaced the note, and went back upstairs and to bed and a disturbed night. He had to make things right for the two of them.

Rafe could have done without a day like the next one. Sondra left early, driving up to visit Millicent. Sue Lee had her phone going to voice mail, Rand had been in early and left for the day. He had said he could not be reached for a few hours, that Miss Powell would be their contact. If needed. All of that caused him to spend a few hot moments. He needed to have Rand present in order to get those records of Lana Jo's and get in touch with the Stamer/Trimble lawyer. And he needed to get back to his own office. He had responsibilities.

Rafe had a private phone number that he had never used. Now was the time. It was not a matter of waiting…now! He said it aloud. He used Rand's private number and placed his call.

"Hello," the voice was soft, hesitant. "Mrs. Womack speaking. May I help you?"

He identified himself and heard her speak to someone who was in the room with her.

Rand said, "Rafe. What's so important you have to call me here? I left a note for Alma. She was supposed to tell everyone I was unavailable. Rafe, this had better be good."

"Oh, man. It is better than good. It is bad, Rand. It is bad." And with that Rafe took about ten minutes to give him the facts. "So, you can see that I need copies of those files on Lana Jo. I will take them to their attorney…yeah, I bet he will still be with them. I think I can turn them off for good, but I do need that stuff."

"And Sondy. Did she believe all that stuff Eveline told her?"

"Not all of it, Rand. But she will have to talk to you about the other. I don't know if it is a lie…it doesn't have anything to do with this…Sondra left for Sac this morning. She is hurting. But it isn't that she put any stock in this lawsuit. She told me emphatically to clear you without a blemish. I will, old man. Just get me these documents, please."

"I'll meet you at the bank on Market Street in twenty minutes. The documents are in a safe deposit box. We can make copies there. I'll go from there back to the office. I thought Sondra would take over while I was out for a couple of days." He hesitated as if deciding something, "my Mom is here, and I had planned to get them together at dinner this evening. I wanted to ask Sondra last night, but…guess that is not going to happen. Twenty minutes, Rafe."

Twenty minutes it was. They came together in tier parking and walked in together. Rafe once again going over his tactics for avoidance of litigation, and Rand giving the go-ahead. Rafe could not help Rand's quiet withdrawal, even though he knew he was partly to blame for keeping Rand and Sondra apart last evening. He did feel a tweak of guilt, briefly.

He finally asked, "Rand, do you think Sondra left because she didn't want to be a part of your problems? She did not…she didn't believe a word of it. Trust me. There was something else—she did say she would back off until she had a talk with you…no, I'm not at liberty to say, Rand. Call her, find her. She loves you, man. Don't let it fester between you."

Rand held the bank's access door and they went in. It took only a few moments to complete their business and Rafe left with his briefcase loaded with dynamite. There was no way that family could disclaim these medical facilities.

Some of the biggest in the nation. He was confident that he had their lawsuit closed before it opened. Rand had even had both folders notarized, as Rafe once suggested. "This will take care of it Rand. It's as good as done. Now you get to Sondra as soon as possible and have that talk."

Rafe left Rand at the deposit box, hurried back to his car, and went directly to Powell Imports to the office and made some calls. With satisfaction, he had an appointment to meet with the Stamer/Trimble attorney, who stated he had been trying to reach Rafe on that very subject.

They met in a quiet lounge downtown and found a secluded table. To anyone looking they were a couple of businessmen with briefcases having a friendly drink. Joseph Braxton was already expressing concern about the Trimble accusation; he had understood that Lana Jo had MS from an early age. Now this. He could find no record of any questionable behavior on Rand's part. He would be happy to clear this up right away. Before his clients got hit with attempted defamation of character charges. He signed a receipt, accepted the copies of the files and promised to return them to Rafe as soon as he could. He would have them recorded, sealed and leave a statement that would block anyone from filing for the family in the future.

"I didn't like this from the *git-go*, Rafe. That bunch wants to sue for every little thing. Not into working for a living. As it is, they won't pay me a dime, because I didn't get them what they wanted. Money."

"Just so they don't sue you, Joe. Good luck to you. It's been a pleasure. Drinks on me."

"Good job, man. Everts owes you plenty. Don't know him, hear he is keen on integrity."

"He is that," Rafe admitted as he took his leave. "And a great deal more."

That evening, Rafe returned to Powell House for dinner; Rand had not returned. Of course he'd want to spend time with Selena. He always took her to concerts, and they often visited a rescue mission and helped there for several hours. And they loved walking on the beach, which required them to drive a few miles north to a friend's property with ocean beach. Suddenly, Rafe wondered why Rand had not brought his mother and Sondra together yet…and then he knew without a doubt what was happening. Rand was always gallantly protective of Selena. But soon…

He was getting ready for bed, packing and laughing his head off. He decided on a drink to help him sleep and went downstairs barefoot to mix a gin and tonic. He sipped it slowly in the darkened library until he had it consumed, standing at the window and looking out at the night. "What a mess. Rand seeing a woman? Of course. His mom. I never thought of it. And if he hasn't shared with Sondra yet, she'll never put two and two together. Well you guys, you straighten that one out. I've done mine…I'll call her tomorrow about the meeting today."

He set the glass on the corner of the desk and went to his room, undressed and got into bed. He stared at the ceiling, pulled up the covers, put the light out and went to sleep.

Sondra arrived in Sacramento after the two hour drive, and found Millicent and Gary still organizing that attic. But it was amazing what they had done. Fortunately the ceiling was well insulated against California heat and now many antiques would grow even older in this setting. They were finishing one last little storage space with hangers, a built in chest all behind a door. When she asked about it, Millicent said, "When our student arrives, he or she will have extra storage. No leaving stuff all over the floors and beds…I cannot tolerate such disarray. It will be understood at once, too."

"You have had word, then, Millie. I haven't been told yet. I suppose it is in my IN basket at work. Have they a candidate? When will he arrive? That's marvelous. Did they tell you what the little bit of allowance would be? Good, I wanted at least two hundred a month. So, that's it for now. You've studied the contract that the student signs…any problems and you let Rafe know immediately. He'll be by to check on you regularly."

"So, how is Sue Lee? I believe you call her Sunny now, she told me on the phone the other day. That's cute, dear. And how is Rand? He hasn't been to see us in a while."

"With James in Argentina, she stays busy. Hard to reach. Rand keeps busy. He does run the business. He is going to Taiwan Wednesday. I was going along, but have decided I needed this time with you. I have had some stressful days lately. This will seem like a little vacation. I thought we could get some tickets to theater, ballet or whatever you would like to do."

"You aren't going to Taiwan? Are you mad, Sondra? That is an opportunity of a lifetime. Think of seeing that beautiful place…you had better think this over carefully."

"He did plan it for us to have the weekend together…something came up Millie. I'll explain later, when you have a minute. For now, I am going to go bake cookies with Alma."

Alma was baking three different recipes for drop cookies. She had ingredients lined up assembly line style and with no little effort the two turned out fifteen dozen cookies that morning. It was part of Alma's job. It was soothing activity for Sondra. Nevertheless, they had finished and were surveying their creativity, three different cookies—seemingly hundreds of them—when Alma shocked Sondra by informing her that now they would pack up twelve dozen in the boxes she got out. They were going to the children's shelter on a quiet street in Oakland.

"Fella named Enoch comes for them. Should be here soon."

"Admirable," Sondra murmured. "It's good we get a taste of them…I'll be in the library. I've a call to make."

Before settling down, she went to the window. How she loved this room. The one in San Francisco was equally as beautiful, but somehow this was the first one…and it meant more to her. Perhaps because her mother had spent much time here. She gazed out at the garden. Rafe had said Rand loved his mother. That was a plus. *I wonder where she is now. Does she know her daughter-in-law is deceased and her family is threatening him? Did she like Lana Jo?*

Sondra turned from the window and went to the desk. She chose the private phone, picked up and called Rand. And her heart sank as the voice mail informed her that he would not be available until his return from Taiwan on Sunday. Until that time any private calls would go to an answering service.

He's returning Saturday? She sat back in the chair. *But he had planned…why he hadn't called her?* "Oh, silly Sondy. You have hurt him. Did he go alone, or take her with him?"

She could not help herself. She called the hotel. Mrs. Womack had checked out this morning. And then Sondra committed the worse crime, yet, by calling Judith Cheney.

Rand had taken Greg Foster, Manager of Acquisitions, with him.

"Well that's nice. I'll be back in next week. Meantime, I'll be working out of the office here. You can reach me by fax or phone. And Judith can you locate Mr. Barker for me. He has some important information for me…he did? I'll call him here then."

"Fine," Sondra muttered, and placed a call to a florist, ordered twelve pink roses sent to Judith Cheney at Powell Imports. Unable to reach Rafe, she waited, and when he called at five-thirty, Sondra invited him to dinner at six, after which he had asked for time with her in the library. He waited there patiently, eyeing the gift box that contained the jade bear in upright stance. It was perfect, Caleb would have been thrilled with it. Presently Sondra joined him with a tray bearing after-dinner coffee. He made a place for it on the coffee table in front of the settee. She frowned at the box.

She poured coffee and they took a few moments to just enjoy the respite.

Finally she asked, "Where did that gift come from, do you know? I don't recall anyone saying anything about it. It has to be you—"

"It's yours. Open it. Don't argue. You will understand in a moment."

"Rafe—" She had it opened in seconds, the bear lifted out and unwrapped from the tissue and all she could say was, "Papa's block of jade. You had it done. It is marvelous. It will live on that same spot forever, only now it has shape and form. Oh, Rafe. How lovely of you to do this."

"You called him Papa."

"Yes, I did. I do sometimes, in my mind. It feels right."

"It is right, Sondra. Caleb hears it, I am sure. He waited a long time for it. So, now we turn to the Rand situation."

And then Rafe explained how he had prevented a law suit that would have ruined Rand Everts. "They were determined. But. Their attorney, Joseph Braxton knows them for what they are. By now it is all sealed up. They can never touch Rand. Anything they try to do about this will get them behind bars…so, Sondra. Rand is safe."

The shine in her eyes for a few seconds was all the thanks he needed. But he wanted desperately to tell her…to ease her heartache. Instead he brought up some import business for an hour before he left her to enjoy her evening with Millicent.

Rafe Barker held his silence in the matter of Rand Everts and a woman.

Chapter Twenty

As if coming to life after a long sleep, everyone was wondering why they had not seen or heard from Sue Lee. With James away, they had expected to see more of her. Sondra had tried four times to reach her, and had even checked out the courthouse. But no one had seen her. There were many suggestions as to where she could be but Sondra knew she had not gone with James. She would have told them if she had decided to follow him...no, something was amiss. Now it was time to call the police and send them to the house. Perhaps Sunny was there, ill or injured and unable to get help. Fear began to grip Sondra and she was unable to shake it off.

She placed a call to the nearest San Francisco Police Department. "SFPD, Officer Boyd Peck," answered her request to speak to someone.

Without hesitation Sondra explained what her concern was, listened as he asked a number of questions, and assured her he would look into it immediately. Judge Powell was special to the members of the force. He would be in touch as soon as he had something to report.

The waiting seemed endless. But Thursday evening she received a call from the officer whom she had contacted. Listening to what she did not want to hear; nevertheless, he informed her that there was evidence of breaking and entry, of forced abduction of Judge Powell. They were beginning a search of the area immediately, and had called in the County Sheriff. "I would advise you to return to San Francisco at your earliest convenience. We will need next of kin on hand, and since Mr. Kwan is out of the country, Judge Powell's sister would suffice."

Sondra found herself shaking and cold. But with Millicent's common sense reasoning that to get in a hurry to write Sue Lee off was silly, Sondra controlled her emotions. And the two of them, two hours later, traveled the freeway for two hours after dark. Thankfully among thinned traffic.

They arrived at Powell House to find a mob of police and media at the front entrance.

Neither spoke. Sondra parked as far up the drive as she could maneuver despite the crowd, and got out. Officer Peck, alerted to their arrival, strode forward, grasped each of them by the arm and ushered them through the horde of people.

"Thank you for your protection," Sondra told him.

A harried Mavis met them in the foyer, asking, "What in the world is it? What has happened? They won't tell me anything but that it concerns a missing member of the family."

Sondra put her arm around the disturbed woman and said, "My sister is missing, Mavis."

"We don't know where Judge Powell is." Officer Peck acknowledged. "We are searching for her. We know she went in to work, the guard verified that, and that she left a little after six that evening. She was chatting animatedly about getting home to a bowl of soup and a relaxing evening with a good book." He hesitated, gazing at them, perhaps considering how much to tell them.

"But—" Sondra prompted.

"We believe she walked into a trap. That he or they were waiting inside for her. The house was trashed; obviously they were looking for something. Nothing was taken as far as we can determine. Perhaps if you could accompany me, and look around to see if you notice anything missing…"

They left immediately, riding in the police car as it sped to Sue Lee's and James' house. Although it was dark, there were lights inside, but only the official cars were there. No media was present, which Sondra gave thanks for. The crowds were intimidating, to say the least.

They started to go inside, and Millicent said, "Sondra can do this, Officer. Perhaps I could be allowed to make a cup of tea. We've driven from Sacramento in the dark…strenuous."

With raised eyebrows, the man said, "not sure that will be possible. The kitchen seemed to be where they expressed their anger…I'll leave you to it, then. Miss Powell, lead the way, please."

Millicent stepped into the new kitchen, and gasped. "Oh, dear Lord!" Anything breakable was broken, anything of any size that could contain edibles was emptied where it stood...

"What could they have wanted, for heaven's sake? And what were they doing to Sue Lee by the time they did this?" Tea was out of the question, and fear and grief caused her to clutch at her chest. She turned and was about to leave for the front porch, when she noticed the dark spots on the floor. Whatever it was had dripped, and then, as if someone were dragging a bulky burden, it was smeared for a couple of feet.

Millicent reached out for the counter to support herself. "I've too vivid an imagination," she murmured and hurried out of the kitchen, down the hall and out onto the porch. She gulped in the fresh air, began to weep, and would have sat down on the porch had not an officer helped her to a bench. Later she was to remember that the young man did not speak. Simply stayed beside her, holding her hand until Sondra returned.

Sondra was not able to find anything missing, but one could not determine what they were looking for. Officer Peck had carefully explained the findings as the investigators tentatively reconstructed the abduction. It was evident that Sue Lee had resisted. It appeared that they dragged her over the entire house...when they came up emptyhanded they moved on, until even the attic had been visited. In that vast space, only one trunk had been stored, and it had family heirlooms from the Kwan family...memories of everything Chinese which were strewn all over.

"They were angry as h—heck, Miss Powell. It looks like they were after something more than jewelry or money. They didn't touch a couple hundred dollars of coins in the den...in a glass vase. They broke the strangest things... can't understand what they thought was here."

As if a voice had spoken to her, Sondra thought, Papa's jade? Cautiously, she collected herself, "Sue Lee was adopted by my parents before I was born. She was mixed race, given over to my father for protection in times when it was frowned upon. They brought the small child home with them from their honeymoon. She had only the clothes on her back. So I would say that lets out anything in connection with what she might have brought with her. I do know that her husband, James Kwan is American. Born here—neither of them brought exaggerated wealth to their marriage...."

Boyd Peck shook his head. "You never know what triggers crime. I have to warn you. I don't have hope of finding her alive. There are too many places in here where blood was spilled. I want to warn you ahead of finding her. I truly hope we do find her alive and well…but—"

"Thank you—."

"Peck!" A breathless young policeman was at the door. "We may need to get an ambulance. The other lady, Mrs. Sherman isn't doing so well…shock, maybe."

"Millie," Sondra said, and made good time getting to her aunt. She was pale and clammy, and kept insisting she was all right. But the shock was evident and Sondra took charge. "Please, do get one here quickly; her pulse is thready…we need her checked out—be still Millie. You are in shock. We'll get help in a minute. Just stay still, and breathe gently. That's my darling…"

The officers parted for the racing vehicle with lights flashing. And they quietly made way again when it left with Millicent and Sondra inside. So, in deference for their behavior, Officer Peck released them and within half an hour only a guard remained at the Kwan home.

Newspapers headlined the story. Television news began with the story, and it was on the lips of many people. Millicent went home to Powell House with Sondra the next day, a little wrung out, but well and healthy.

The search continued, and the wait was agonizing for everyone. Particularly for Sondra who, after an especially disturbing nightmare, had begun to suspect that the two men from China, supposedly searching for the jade, had been at the bottom of this. But how to prove it without setting hordes on a search for that fairy tale jade? Rand had said to let it be. Caleb ordered complete secrecy, would not verify that it was even a true story. But, Rand knew it existed, and he had to know where it was.

"How in the world does one hide ancient jade artifacts? It wasn't in Caleb's personal lock box at the bank…it certainly wasn't anywhere in the house or I would have happened onto it by now. If it was only a tall tale, Sue Lee may have given her life for nothing." She murmured.

Sitting on the side of her bed, she sighed. "I am going mad. I am talking to myself, having horrible dreams, losing the man I love and hating the Caleb Powell legacy. There, I've said it. That doesn't change a thing—I am going for a walk, hoping for a dog soon."

Millicent said from the dark doorway, "That is not really Sondra, is it. Some stranger has taken her over…never heard you talk to yourself like that, my darling. Come on. Let's get some coffee, then maybe we can sleep." She led the way to the kitchen, and turned on the light.

"I will never ever sleep again, Millie. Don't wake Mavis. I am only going to talk to myself from now to eternity."

"Well, after this little hospital episode, I may never reach eternity. I shall never die, but remain on this earth to suffer forever. You know of course, we can never go to hell…we live in it and don't know it"

"Oh, darling Millie. Hush. I'll make the coffee, you make some toast—what on earth! Who can be at the door at this hour…someone with a key?" She grabbed a chef's knife from the block of knives on the counter and turned toward the door to the hall. Footsteps came their way, hesitated and then Rand, burdened by his suitcase, entered the kitchen and stopped.

"You planning to use that on me?"

The dam broke. Sondra sat down on a kitchen chair with a thump. The beautiful room was swimming around and she could not see for the flood of tears. Tentatively she placed the knife on the table beside her and dropped her head to the table and wept her heart out.

Rand looked at Millie, then at Sondra, and back. *What should I do?* His eyes pleaded.

Millicent gestured "Go to her, you lummox. She needs you more than anything. I am going back to bed. With *you* here no one will murder me in my bed."

Rand watched her trundle off to bed in her nightgown. Sondra, he realized was in her pajamas…his heart skipped a beat. He released the luggage and stepped over to her. "Sondra, I didn't mean to scare you to death. I came home as soon as I heard about Sue Lee…I knew you would be needing my presence, regardless of …well I guess something came between us."

She couldn't lift her head. Her nose was running too. "Yes, I'm glad you came. I can't do it all. The company…I have to find Sue Lee. I can't lose her now. We just found each other. She is my sister. I was her maid of honor, now she has to be mine when I get married someday."

She looked up at him, swiped her hand across her nose and wiped it on her pajamas. "You must be tired. Better get up to bed and get some rest. It's no picnic around here. You have flown a long way to come home to this chaos. Go to bed Rand. That's where I am going."

She left him standing there, her image in those pajamas so vivid that he gasped and would have grabbed himself. He had not had a physical reaction like that in his life.

"Whew!" he said, took up his Samsonite and turned out the light and went up to bed.

When the authorities gave Sondra permission to clean up Kwan's house before James returned, she avoided going in to the office. Rand was there and didn't really need her, she told herself. He stayed on in the house, they had dinner with everyone else as usual, but with the somber note over everything, they were a subdued bunch. He had to put up with it all. He loved her and had to be there for her. She was going to be hard-hit when they found Sue Lee. There was no way he could discuss anything with her…she was distant and grieving, and he couldn't intrude there. Not on his life. If she were his, he could hold her, make love to her and ease her pain…but…no.

The Kwan's home was almost restored when James came home, unexpectedly. He went into his house and found Sondra, Mavis and Millicent supervising the replacement of breakables, and non-breakables. He was horrified… what had happened to his house. Where was his bride? She was supposed to pick him up at the airport. She didn't answer her mobile.

Mavis and Millicent left for home. Sondra and James went into the den and for hours they sat while Sondra told him everything, except her suspicion of two men from Asia and the jade. She merely pointed out that they did not know for certain what the motive was. His grief was guarded for a while. Soon, he let it overcome him. "They have got to find her, Sondra. I can't live without her. What did they want with her? They should send her home now. I need her."

At last they wept together, unable to hold off any longer. James paced, began touching the desk, and a chair, and the books. He opened her desk drawer. All was in order as Sue Lee kept it. He shut it soundly.

"Oh, James. We have to wait. I just know they *will* find her soon. You must get in touch with your family. They can help you wait this out. Promise me? And you have got to stay close, if you will.…"

"Yeah, sure, Sondra. Sure, they will be sad. They love her.…"

The body of Sue Lee Powell Kwan was found on a Sacramento levee, at three in the afternoon on a Saturday by two teenage boys who were exercising their dogs. The search was over, but the grief was just beginning for those who loved her. Her life had not been one of assurances, but of struggle to be a person who despite her background was able to give and not take from society with her capability to judge. That she chose to be an American was notable, and noble to many who knew her. After all her mother was English, and her father had been someone of importance in China. She might have demanded more of life, but Caleb Powell had made the right decisions in her life. She had grown up to her full potential. Giving back to society. Her life ended too soon.

The two boys who found her on the levee had made the trip by bike, parked them and when the dogs scampered down to get a drink of water after the thirsty run, they had stumbled on the body in the grass at the edge of the river. One boy remained behind with the dogs, while the other went for help. Of all things told to him, James Kwan was grateful for the boy who stayed to protect her from any further harm.

James was numb when they notified him. He'd gone to identify his beautiful wife and would forever remember the bludgeoned body that made him hesitate because it did not look like Sue Lee, and he wanted still to hope that she was alive somewhere.

"He's in denial," many people said. But were helpless when he rebuffed their attempts to placate him. "When they find the killers," he often said, "I will know that she is with them, being held against her will."

Everything now fell to him. He received the coroner's report, the death certificates, made the arrangements and went home to his empty house every day in a stupor. His mother told him, "Numbness is a blessing, because when it was over you will have pain for many years which will cause you to wish for relief in any form. You cannot do anything about it, my son."

James tried not to go mad as they waited for the investigation to be over and Sue Lee's killers to be apprehended. However, in ten days, her remains were released and he completed the preparations to lay her to rest. It would be years before he could remember any of the details.

Millicent was somewhat resigned, and Sondra had not reconciled to the evil person who caused Sunny's death for whatever reason drove such an act. In her mind, she was convinced it was that pair who had been adamant about the jade artifact. There had been something about them…the more she had to push those thoughts away, the more they filled her mind.

The day of the funeral, Sondra found Rand in the library of Powell House and closed the door and leaned against it. "Now, we are going to settle some things, Rand Everts." She took a seat in one of the big chairs. "Sit." She waited, as he frowned, and chose the big accent chair and sat.

"Good dog?" he asked.

"Hush. We have to settle something before we leave for the service. Rand, I think Sunny was killed because they thought she had that jade thing, whatever it is. No, now listen.…" She told him about the two men who had visited her, and again when she was away. How adamant they had been that it actually existed. "They wanted that jade, Rand. Sunny didn't even know about it,"

Rand looked startled. "I don't think they—"

"Rand, where is it? I am sure you know where it is. I want it. It must go with Sue Lee Kwan, in her casket. To rest forever. No one must ever know… but you have to give it to me."

"But if they didn't get it from her, they will be back, surely."

"They can't. I told Officer Peck about them, and he turned it over to the FBI."

Chapter Twenty One

Rand stood up. He went over to the bookcase and stretched to reach the top shelf. When he straightened, he had the strange looking stone, or geode…but he turned it around—the bottom was flat. He took out his pocket knife, snapped off a cover which was so cleverly designed it did not appear removable. One had to know….

Nestled in the hollow, in a silk lining, was a white jade artifact, pure and exquisite of some mythical figure known only to the artist. It was animal, or human combined?

"This carving is pure white jade, from the Ch'ing Dynasty which existed from sixteen forty-four to nineteen twelve A.D. Caleb said: 'this was the greatest period for jade carvings. There were two emperors who promoted the artists, and many beautiful pieces were done in nephrite—pure jade being more rare. This was passed down to Su Liu's father, a Mandarin whose name was Disih Fu Hao. He knew the new government would take it from him, as they were taking everything. The child was not the only reason he asked me to take her…this sculpture was her heritage.' "Those were Caleb's words," Rand concluded.

Sondra went over to look at the jade, she reached out to touch it. "It is so old, Rand—so old! It must be worth a fortune."

"There are collectors, yes, who would pay millions or more for it. But to offer it up would bring that country down on our heads as well as every crook in the world. It is priceless. I don't know if I agree that it should go with her…maybe you are right. We should get rid of it once and for all. But will that assure your safety? And your family's safety when you have children? Give me a minute to think."

"Great art should never be destroyed, I know. But this one I am certain now, is revealed, and dangerous to everyone. Perhaps we should return it to their museum...."

"I don't like that idea. It might be too dangerous...."

"Give it to me, in the shell. It goes with Su Liu. It's hers. She bought it with her life."

Rand did not fail to hear her use of the oriental name one last time.

And, so, Papa's jade went with Sunny who had paid the supreme price for it. Sondra managed a final moment with Sue Lee at a private viewing, where she quickly tucked the silk-wrapped package down beside her sister in in a fold of the silk-lined casket. Then she insisted they seal the casket at that moment, she stayed with it to the grave, and waited until the earth was placed over it. And then she turned, took Rand's arm and went home to her grief.

No one had questioned her actions, in fact there was admiration that she loved Sue Lee so deeply, after so many years apart. No one would question the colorful shopping bag she had carried, no one spoke of it.

Rand did not leave her for several days. She slept in his arms, she talked to him, going over her sadness, and he loved her unreservedly.

Millicent paced like a cat, in and out, hardly weeping, until one day she said, "Well that's enough. Nothing is going to change. It is over, it is done. Caleb, what a monster you set into motion with your desire to open trade with China. Wherever you are, I wonder if you know what the outcome has been, the effect on so many people. Goodbye, Caleb." And with that, Millie went to the kitchen and chopped vegetables for a salad, to Mavis' surprise.

Millicent traveled back to Sacramento with Alma and Merilee who had come for the funeral and were going back. As they sped over the highway, and with a heavy heart, she began to turn her thoughts to her new resident. She'd reared a girl, now how was it going to be to live with a young man in that mansion in Sacramento? Did she still have it in her, she wondered.

Having wondered out loud brought a response from Alma, "Oh, but you will love it. I've got several grandsons, and they are so much easier than girls. Of course, if you have any problems I will be very happy to help, or give advice."

Merilee, who was driving, complained, "I didn't give you trouble."

"So you say," Alma retorted, lowered her window and let the breeze beat her hair to a tangled mop.

Sorrow at bay a few weeks later, and Rand and Sondra did finally communicate. Rand was totally puzzled that Sondra held him at arm's length. He was about to give it up and go to ranching with the Womack's. He couldn't stay in her presence and not love her...He had to make one last attempt, though, and chose a mid-morning break at the office to begin feeling around for an approach.

"What was it we needed to talk about, Sondra?" He asked as casually as possible.

It was obvious that they were simply going through the motions of working. He could not wait longer. He wanted her more that he had never dreamed possible. If he was to have a future, it had to be with her.

She studied him over the paperwork on her desk. She got up and came to stand before him. "I know about the woman you have been seeing all these years. But I don't understand why you haven't brought her to meet us. You must love her...are you married to her? What—"

"I'm not seeing—"

"I know she exists. I called the hotel and Selene Womack was there with you. They told me you were together...."

Incredulous, Rand couldn't get his mind to respond. He began to laugh. Suddenly it was not funny at all. He stood up, excited.

"Sondra, my darling, whom I love more than anyone on earth, I was talking to my *mother*. Selena Everts Womack is actually my stepmother...she raised me from infancy. My mother died at my birth and dad married her when I was just a year old. Later, Dad developed Alzheimer's. She took care of him, and when he died she needed someone to care for her until she married Andrew Womack. She lives in Texas with him, comes to visit when she can."

"Oh. My goodness. You never said...your mother." She felt her flush to her toes.

She said the first thing that came to mind, "so how will she feel about a dog and maybe two kids?"

Rand couldn't move fast enough. He had her fast against him. His heart was racing. "She'll be delighted."

"Me, too." Said Sondra, wrapping her arms around his neck, at last.

Sondra Gaye Powell and Randall Willis Everts were married a year later in the same chapel where Sue Lee had married James. She chose not to wear Hilda Powell's gown, rather she sent it to a museum. Sondra's wedding gown was the lavender maid of honor frock and hat, worn in memory of the wedding of her sister, Sue Lee. It had settled on her body with a warmth at the memory and she felt every bit the elegance she portrayed. And when Rand kissed her at the end of the ceremony, he had pushed up the hat with a smile. Sondra re-settled it when he whispered "Mrs. Everts. My love." She held it as they ran down the aisle and out the door into the sunshine.

Their wedding rings were traditional diamonds in white gold mountings. "Nothing pretentious," she had insisted, "just binding us together. And warding off intruders."

James Kwan gave the bride away, and Rafe Barker was best man, and the chapel was filled with friends of both bride and groom. Aunt Millicent, Serena and Andrew Womack and Gem Chang sat together at the front of the chapel and whispered to one another, much to the distress of the pastor. Alma and Merilee were bridal attendants, and were delighted to see themselves written up in the Standard Examiner as members of such an auspicious wedding.

Their reception held in Weddings Unlimited hall was attended by most of Powell Import's employees, and seven employees from SG Interior Designs were flown in for the event. Trystan Millerson and Afton Van Alt got high on champagne and sang a raucous duet to the pair.

Sondra's wedding gift to Rand was a document making him co-owner of Powell Imports.

Rand gave his bride a spaniel puppy, and their first child, due nine months later. And an exquisite ring of smoky blue chalcedony surrounded by diamonds, in white gold.

Papa's jade went into oblivion.

It took only a month for Sondra to have her final wish. It happened when they were snug in the bed where they often shared their deepest longings, quietly, privately.

"Rand."

"Hm. I'm nearly asleep. What is it, my heart?"

"Rand, I noticed a very derelict Victorian house the other day up on Highway 80 out of Sacramento. It had a for sale sign on it. Do you think I could look into it? With you in charge of Powell Imports I could restore it using my company."

"Uh, huh. Sure. Sound idea. I was just waiting for you to ask, I knew you had seen it…so I bought it. You can get to work on it when you are ready. Papers are in order, permits taken care of…Judith will have everything handy for you."

Sondra reared up, leaving him uncovered, "You did what?"

Rand yawned, pulled her close and felt the covers settle over them. "I bought it last week. It's all yours, love."

She snuggled closer, "I wonder if Gary Toppel is available."

Rand laughed, "Give him a call. He's waiting for it."

"Husband, you know me so well, don't you. My father saw to that, I guess."

"Well I suppose I could do some serious explaining, in case there is something I missed."

"You're good, you know that. You never miss…."

"Not with you, I don't miss."

"Rand, you had better not be *explaining* to anyone else,"

"Never," he laughed, and wrapped himself around her. "You are all the territory I can afford forever."

Sondra let him have the last word, just this once.

The End